Nice for what?

RECIE D.

To Stefanie
Thank you for the support
Enjoy the read !! :)

Recie D.

Prologue

I stood on the rooftop, looking down at the world below me. Blurred lights speeding by made me dizzy. I looked forward and closed my eyes as the cool night air brushed my face. I held my head between my hands; I could feel myself unsteadily stumbling forward. *Why am I feeling so impaired?* That was the only question running through my mind as I held on to the ledge. I only had a few drinks, and they were pretty watered down. I opened my eyes, staring down, and the swirling lights continued to make me feel lightheaded. I turned around and perched myself slightly on the ledge, just enough to where I could rest but still keep my feet on the ground.

"Lina!" I heard a voice yell loudly, startling me so much that I lost my balance. Suddenly, I felt like a lightweight. *I'm falling.*

RECIE D.

(Two Weeks Before)

Darlina Long (Friday Morning)

I stood naked in front of my full-length mirror, examining my body. I stood a full five feet four, 180 pounds, and my breasts hung slightly. My hourglass waist made up for that though. I turned to the side and looked at my average-sized butt. Some days, I wished it was a little bigger, but overall, it did its justice. My milk-chocolate skin glistened from the Shea butter that I'd just applied. I reached over and grabbed the wide-toothed comb and started to untangle my wet, curly, shoulder-length hair. I heard the shower shut off, and within minutes, my husband, Adrian, emerged from the bathroom with a towel wrapped around his waist.

"How was the shower, AJ?" I asked in a cheerful tone.

"When are you getting your straight hair back?" he replied abrasively, ignoring my question.

"Well, I thought it would be nice to give my hair a little break and wear it natural for a few weeks, bae." I grabbed the brush and swept my hair up into a high, bushy ponytail and then started working on my edges. I directed my gaze at him through the mirror. "You can't tell me that this isn't cute," I said playfully, trying to ease the tension in the room.

"It's not," he said dryly without even looking up. I watched him as he oiled his muscular frame with Shea butter; the oil made his smooth peanut butter skin glow deliciously. He stood up to a full six feet four. Sometimes, I couldn't understand how someone so fine could be so mean. I finished up my hair and walked over to the bed and started to put on my bra and panties.

He walked to the opposite side of the bed and started to get dressed as well. The room was silent, and the shifting from the clothes made it even more awkward. Finally, I could feel his judging eyes glaring at me. I looked up, realizing that I didn't have the energy or the time to spark up a debate. I let out a soft sigh.

"I'll make an appointment to get my hair done." My tone mirrored my feelings of defeat. I turned around, facing the wall, and pulled my scrub bottoms up. "Do you mind handing me my top, or is that too much to ask?" I asked in a snappier tone than I wanted to give off. I could hear him laugh as he walked over to me, caressed my back for a moment, and then helped me pull my shirt over my head.

He wrapped his arms around my waist and pulled me closely. "Babe," he started in a soft tone. "I'm sorry. I'm not trying to offend you; it's just that kinky hair—"

I cut him off. "Yeah, I know. It's not a part of the Long

2

image." I used my fingers as quotation marks as I quoted his family's favorite line. He gently turned me around. I stared in his brown eyes, and he smiled and kissed me on the forehead.

"I knew you would understand," he said approvingly. He let me go and continued to gather his things for work. "I have to get to the firm, baby," he added as he hurried to the door. "Hey, bae."

"Yes?" I replied.

"Try to get to the gym sometime this week." That was his final jab before walking out of the room. I heard his footsteps head down the stairs and the front door close behind him.

Looking in the mirror at myself, I sighed. I knew I had gained a few extra pounds since the wedding, but I honestly thought it filled me out quite nicely. I shook my head, slipped on my work shoes, and walked out the room, down the stairs, and into the kitchen. I reached for a croissant but decided on an apple instead.

"Don't want to offend him by gaining any more weight," I mumbled to myself as I left out the house to head to work.

Adrian Long Jr.

I opened the door to my black new hotness and slid into my nice, chocolate, leather seats. I started the engine and pulled out of the driveway. In my rearview, I could see Lina walking out of the house and getting into her car. *She could really walk to work,* I thought but quickly shook that spirit of downing my wife out of my mind. She had gained a few pounds since the wedding last year, but that wasn't a reason for me to be so rude to her this morning. Thicker women just weren't my thing, and I hoped that she took my advice and hit the gym. *I need the slim chick I married back.* My thoughts were cut off by my phone ringing. My buddy Nathan's name popped up on the screen. I answered through the car's Bluetooth.

"What up, Nate?"

"Aye, my nigga, where are you?"

"I just left the house. Me and Lina was having a conversation that ran longer than I thought it would," I said as I thought back to the events of my morning. "She had the nerve to leave out the house with that natural shit on her head," I said with a laugh.

"Black power!" Nate replied jokingly.

"Yeah, ight, forget that shit. I like that long, straight hair," I said as I started to reminisce about the Lina from back in the day— slim with long hair, perky titties, and tight ass waist. *Damn.* I licked my lips before being pulled out of my trance.

"Aye, motherfucker, do you hear me!" Nate yelled through

the speaker. I laughed as I pulled into my firm's parking lot.

"No, I didn't, but I'm about to head up to the office now."

"Wait—" I heard him start up, but I hung up before he could finish. *Oops. I hope he wasn't saying anything important,* I thought as I turned off the engine and got out of the car.

I walked into the building and stopped in my tracks. There was a fine ass woman standing at the receptionist's desk. She wasn't facing me, but I knew with a body like that, she had to be beautiful. She was about five feet six with long legs, a tight booty, and a narrow waist. She had long hair hanging down to the middle of her back. I licked my lips and was about to make my move when she turned around.

"Adrian!" the familiar voice yelled out, and I realized it was an old friend from college.

"Hazel, girl, is that you?" I asked as I embraced her in a quick hug.

"How are you?" she asked with a big smile on her face. She was still as pretty as she was in college—dark-chocolate skin, a big, pretty smile complemented with pearly white teeth, a cute little nose, and big, hazel eyes. She was perfection.

"What are you doing here?" I asked, looking her up and down.

"I work here now!" she exclaimed with a smile. "It's going to be like old times, us working on cases together. I'm very excited!" she exclaimed. I was about to say something, but I saw Nate out of the corner of my eye, and he was waving for me to come over.

"I'm excited as well. I know with you in the building, things are going to be handled well. Go ahead and get settled, and I'll catch up with you later," I said as I hugged her once more. I turned around and quickly walked into Nate's office, closing the door behind me. "Nigga, what the fuck is Hazel doing here?" I asked in an uneasy tone.

"My nigga, that's what I was trying to tell your ass on the phone. She showed up this morning, saying your father hired her." I looked at him in disbelief.

"My father?" I repeated and then shook my head. "This nigga." *I should have known this was his doing.* "I am going to have to speak to him about this."

"Yeah, but that's going to have to wait until later because a big case just landed in our hands, and we really have to get to work." I really wanted to confront my father right now, but business always came first.

Lina

I pulled into the parking lot of the hospital where I worked. I looked at the clock; I had about ten minutes until I really needed to go in. I sat there, eating my apple, thinking about the events that transpired this morning. I loved my husband, but I hated having to fit into the mold of his expectations. I continued to sit and eat the apple, even though my stomach growled heavily for pancakes. I didn't know where this increased appetite was really coming from, but I did know that the more down I felt, the hungrier I got. *Am I an emotional eater?* I wondered as my mind recalled all my eating moments. *No, I don't have an eating problem. I'm just married now, and I do a lot of cooking.* My mind wandered to all the new meals that I found on Facebook and cooked for AJ, just trying to be a good wife. *Damn, am I a good wife?* I sat there, doubting myself, as I continued to munch on the apple.

I was startled by a tap on my window followed by a loud, flamboyant, "Biiiiiitttch!" I smiled when I looked up and saw my best friend Oliver. He had a big smile on his face and was holding up two bags from Dunkin' Donuts. I turned off the engine, grabbed my purse, and hopped out of the car. "Girl, what the hell is you doing with that apple?" His bantering tone made me laugh.

"Man, forget you. I'm trying to stay fit."

"Fit? Bitch, you better fit"—he paused for dramatic effect— "one of these croissant sandwiches in your mouth." He continued by rolling his neck and handing me one of the bags. I

7

loved my best friend Ollie; we'd been friends since high school. He was a little bit taller than me with the perfect golden-brown complexion. He had hazel eyes and he damn near reminded me of that singer Ginuwine. Honestly, he was every woman's dream; too bad he played for the opposite team.

We walked into the building and went our separate ways. Ollie was a nurse, so he went to do his rounds. I was an occupational therapist, so I walked into the OT office and put my food down on my desk. I grabbed my schedule to see how my day was looking. I had two appointments this morning with some of my favorite patients.

"Seems like you have an easy day." I looked back and saw my girl Riley peeking into my food bag. She smiled at me, and all I could see was those deep dimples on her slim, light-skinned face.

"Excuse you," I said as I jokingly pulled the bag from her. I opened the bag and grabbed the bacon, egg, and cheese croissant. The scent was heavenly, and I knew it was about to be so damn good. I was just about to unwrap it completely and indulge in greasy happiness, but my mind quickly thought back to earlier and how I really needed to start watching what I eat. "You know what?" I wrapped the sandwich up and handed it to Riley. "You can have it."

She looked at me weird as she grabbed it. "Why? What's going on?" I could hear the concern in her voice.

"Nothing. I'm just trying to watch my weight," I replied, not wanting to get into the whole *I need to lose weight to keep my man happy* conversation.

"Your what?" I looked back to see my girl Samantha standing in the office doorway next to her med cart.

"My weight, girl. You see I'm getting thicker than a snicker," I replied as she put her things on my desk and looked at me and laughed.

"Girl, it's about time you got a little body on you." Sam walked over, pulled me up from the chair, and spun me around. "Too bad you still ain't got a booty." I looked at her with a stale face, and we all started laughing.

"Yeah, whatever, bitch. Can't everybody have a cornbread and cabbage fed booty like you," I said as Sam did a little twerk routine. Sam was the curviest of our little crew. She was blessed in all the right places, and it matched so well with her russet-brown skin.

"Yeah, I know." She dropped it like it was hot but missed a step and landed right on that big ol' booty.

"Someone is getting old." I laughed while helping her off the floor.

"I'm not old, bitch, just a little out of shape," Sam defended, dusting her butt off.

"Girl, how about we go to the gym after work tonight?" I asked, and both of them looked at me crazy.

"The gym?" Sam blurted out. "I'm good love, enjoy," she said, quoting one of those infamous Twitter memes.

"I'll go with you, Lina. I need to do some squats to plump

9

up this booty," Riley said as she tooted her back up. I say back because Riley was slim and had no booty at all. The only thing big on her was her double D breast.

"On second thought, I will be joining y'all. I have to see what type of miracle squats you about to be doing to get a booty," Sam said, and we all burst with laughter. I loved these girls, and I was so happy and blessed to have them in my life.

Samantha Campbell

I stood at my nursing cart, placing medicine in a little cup for my patient to take. I was just about to walk in the room to give them to her when I received a text message. I looked at my phone, and it was a group text between Riley, Ollie, and I.

Riley: I think something is wrong with Lina

Ollie: Why you say that?

Me: She has been acting a little weird today, not eating her breakfast

Ollie: The breakfast I gave her (shocked emoji)

Riley: It didn't go to waste Ollie and it was good

I put the phone down and went into speed mode to pass out my meds so I could go talk to Lina before Phil and Lil' got to her. I did notice a change in her aura today. Even though she was smiling and laughing, deep down, I could tell something was bothering her. All this talk about her weight, going to the gym, and then refusing to go out for lunch, I could definitely feel it had something to do with that motherfucker Adrian. Ever since she met him in college, she'd been becoming less like her and more like a puppet. I walked in and out of my patients' rooms, making sure they were good, all while trying to keep up with the numerous back and forth messages of endless theories of what could be wrong with her. I knew I had to check in with my girl, but the only way to do that was to finish up my med pass.

Adrian

I was sitting at my desk, looking over some papers, when I heard a knock on the door. Before I could answer, in walked my father, Adrian Sr., with a big grin on his face. "Hey, son." I could tell by his tone, he felt like he did something good.

"Don't *hey, son* me. Why in the hell would you—"

"Excuse me?" he sharply cut me off. His deepened tone let me know I had crossed a boundary.

"I'm sorry, sir, but, Dad, why did you hire Hazel?"

"She needed a job, son," he said amusingly. I couldn't believe he thought this was funny. He knows the history between that girl and me, and I couldn't help but think this was one of his scheming ploys for me to follow in his footsteps.

"Well, can you at least send her to another one of your buildings Dad?" I pleaded.

"No, I cannot son. I am doing this for you." *I knew it; here we go with the Long legacy bullshit.* "Your mother and I always liked Hazel—" he started, but I cut him off.

"No Dad. You guys just like the fact that her family has old money." He looked at me with a serious face. He hated when I cut him off.

"As I was saying, son, you and Hazel were such a great couple. She fit into the mold just perfectly. She's beautiful, well spoken, a hard worker, and yes, it doesn't hurt that she already has her own money unlike—" I cut him off again.

"Unlike who, Dad?" I could feel my face tensing up.

"Cut me off again, and today will be your last day!" my father roared at me like I was a kid that had just did something wrong. The room fell silent for a moment. "Sorry, son," he said, straightening his tie. "But as I was saying, you married that girl that comes from a poor family and has no real sense of worth. She can't help build with you. All she can do is take from you, and that's not the type of woman we need in the line of Long women."

I glared at him angrily. "So, you saying I made the wrong choice in marrying Lina?"

"No. You said that. All I'm saying is that maybe you should've thought with your top head and not your bottom one." He paused. "Either way, Hazel stays, and I'm going to be putting you two on a few cases together, so don't let me down, son." And with that being said, he exited out of my office.

I closed the door, walked to my desk, and angrily knocked the pen holder across the room. *Why would he put me in this situation?* I asked myself, and then I heard a knock on the door. I quickly gathered myself. "Come in," I said in a calm voice, and in walked Aaron.

"Hey, man, are you OK?" I could hear the concern in his voice.

"Yeah, man, just a slight misunderstanding with my pops. Shit will be good though."

"Ight, man. Well, I just came in here to let you know Lina was holding on line three. Someone had transferred her call to my office, so I just wanted to let you know." I really didn't want to talk to her after all this, but I walked to the phone anyway.

"Thanks, bro," I said to Aaron. He nodded and left the office, and I picked up the call.

Lina

I patiently waited on the line for AJ to answer. "Hello?"

"Hey, baby," I replied.

"Who is this?" I heard the voice over the phone ask with a laugh, and I realized it wasn't Adrian.

"Oh, I'm sorry. I thought I was transferred to Adrian Long's office."

"Oh, hey, Darlina. This is Aaron. We have a new receptionist, so she might have gotten the lines confused."

"Hey, Aaron, how have you been?" I asked, not really caring but trying not to make it awkward.

"I've been pretty good." He paused, and it was quiet for a moment. "AJ is in a meeting with his dad right now, but it looks as though it's ending. Just hold the line, and I will get you to him."

"Thank you," I said as the line clicked, and I was back on hold, listening to the smooth jazz. A few minutes went past, and I was getting ready to hang up when I heard the line click over.

"Hey, babe." I could instantly hear the frustration in his voice.

"Hey, sweetie, what's wrong?" I asked, concerningly.

"Nothing, just had a little dispute with my dad; that's all."

"Well, I got a little time. Do you want to talk about it?"

"Naw, babe, I don't really want to get into it, and plus, I'm busy," he said, but I could tell he was distracted.

"OK, well, I was thinking since it's Friday, we should go out tonight and maybe get some drinks and do some dancing. How does that sound?" The line was silent. "Hello? Did you hear me?" I asked as I listened closely in the background to see what was so distracting.

"Oh, yeah, babe, I hear you. That sounds good. Just send me the address to the spot, and I will meet you there around eight." I smiled hard.

"Cool, bae. I can't wait—" I was about to continue, but he cut me off.

"Lina, I have to go. Something has come up."

"OK, I love—" I was cut off by the dial tone. *Well, damn. Fuck you too then,* I thought as I placed my cell phone on the desk.

I stared at the phone, waiting to at least see a text message from him, apologizing and saying he loved me, but nothing came.

"Hey, boo." I was startled out of my thoughts by Sam walking into the room.

"Hey, girl." I tried forcing a smile.

"Lina," she started as she sat next to me. "What the hell is going on?" Her voice was full of worry.

"Nothing," I lied.

"Darlina, stop with the bull. You've been in a slump all day. Wassup?"

I sat, thinking about the moments of my day and deciding on if I really wanted my friends in my business. They never really liked AJ, and I didn't want to deal with an *I told you so*.

"Adrian and I have been in a weird place, but that's all going to change because we are going on a date tonight, and it's going to be the start of us getting on the same page." I rushed through the entire statement and then smiled big. Sam looked at me for a moment, and I could tell she was contemplating on saying something, but then she smiled back.

"OK, girl, I hope you two have a great time." Her tone was unconvincing, but I didn't let it bother me. Tonight was going to be the beginning of something great.

Adrian

I picked up the phone with Lina, trying not to break down. "Hey, babe." I didn't know why, but my dad always got under my skin and made me feel like I was still a little ass kid.

"Hey, sweetie. What's wrong?" Her voice was so sweet over the phone; it made me remember why I fell in love with her in the first place. She truly cared about me as a man. I glanced up for a moment and saw Hazel bending over a desk, looking at some paperwork with Aaron.

"Nothing, just had a little dispute with my dad; that's all." I looked down at my desk, trying to find some paperwork to distract me, but the only thing I could think about was Hazel. I glanced back up.

"Well, I got a little time. Do you want to talk about it?"

"Naw, babe, I don't really want to get into it, and plus, I'm busy," I said as I glared at Hazel's sideway profile. Those long, brown legs were so sexy. I remembered having them wrapped around my neck. Her calves still looked tight from when she used to run track. Her petite booty looked really good in that pinstripe skirt she was wearing. I just wanted to go over there and squeeze it.

"Hello? Did you hear me?"

"Oh, yeah, babe, that sounds good. Just send me the address to the spot, and I will meet you there around eight," I said as Hazel caught my glare. She stood up straight, smiled, waved, and then walked back to her desk. Her perky breast bounced perfectly with every step. I slowly started to caress my growing member. I held back a groan, realizing I was still on the phone with Lina. She was saying something, but I cut her off. "Lina, I have to go. Something has come up." I quickly hung up the phone.

I sat there, trying to calm myself down; Hazel working here was going to be a big problem because sexually, I couldn't control myself. Visions of our late-night creeping in college kept flashing through my head. She would have probably been my wife if she didn't leave in the middle of our third year. After that, I started talking to Lina, and the rest was pretty much history, and I was happy. But since my dad always had to meddle in my life, I was now put in a weird ass predicament.

Lina

I couldn't wait until tonight, I thought as I glanced at the clock. Five o'clock, quitting time and it couldn't have gotten here fast enough. *Tonight, I'm gonna dance for you, ohhh, ohhh.* I hummed the Beyoncé song in my head as I walked to the time clock. I waved goodbye to the crew and headed home. Once I walked through the door, I instantly started to undress. *I didn't have any time to waste.* I thought as I jumped in the shower, making sure to use the smell goods that AJ liked the most. I even did a quick trim on Ms. Wet Wet. *Tonight's going to be the night I swerve on that thing.*

It'd been a minute since AJ and I had sex. Our schedules kept us busy and tired, but tonight... tonight, I was going to let him get all up in this. I hopped out the shower with pep in my step, turned the radio on, and instantly started to move my body to the music. I turned on my flat iron and ran down the stairs to the kitchen. *I need to get lit,* I thought to myself as I grabbed a glass and put it under the ice machine on the fridge. *Just a few cubes.* I did a little booty shake as I jammed to Rhianna's "Work." I pulled open the fridge doors and pulled out the sprite and tequila and started to mix a little drink. *Te'kiki brings out the freak freak.* I chuckled at that saying because it was something Sam and I used to say back in our low key hoe years.

I grabbed my little drink and ran back upstairs. I sipped a little bit and then started to do my hair. He wanted it long, so I was going to give it to him. I looked in the mirror as I straightened my hair with the flat iron. I mean, it wasn't the weaves he loved, but for now, it would do. I took another sip and thought about the first time AJ saw me without weave.

I was sitting in my dorm room, watching reality TV through the mirror as I cut and pulled out the long tracks of hair. I heard a knock on the door, and I figured it was Sam because she always left her keys. "It's open!" I yelled, and I could hear the door open and close. "Girl, how you leave your keys again?" I asked as I pulled out another track and threw it in a plastic bag. "Sam?" I called in a lingering tone as I slowly turned around to see AJ standing there with his mouth wide open.

"Hey, sexy. I didn't know you were coming by," I said as I looked back at the mirror, cutting the thread to release another track. I looked back at AJ, who still stood there with this shocked look on his face. "What's wrong, babe?" I asked as I jumped up, concerned that maybe something had happened. Then I noticed he was looking at my head, and that's when I realized he had never seen me without my weave in, and I guess I did look a little crazy with half my head braided while the other half just hung loosely. "Babe, it's weave." I laughed.

"B-But," he stammered. "I thought that was all you."

"Yeah, that's the point, but no, babe, it's not."

"Woooooooow," he said as if this whole time, I had been telling him a lie.

"Do not overthink it." I laughed and sat back down to finish.

I laughed at the good times while staring in the mirror, finishing up my hair. I hadn't had a perm in years, so it wasn't bone straight like the weave, but it was cute. I put on lotion and opened the closet to pull out this sexy, royal-blue dress. I slipped it on and walked over to the mirror. This was my first time wearing it because when I bought it, it was too big, but now it fit perfectly. The front was a nice lowcut, and my boobs were sitting pretty. I turned around in the mirror. The dress had a dipped back that stopped right on top of my cute bumper booty and a golden backdrop necklace that hung down to the middle of my back. I did a little twerk in the mirror. *Damn, I look good as fuck.*

I grabbed my drink off the dresser and finished it up. I picked up the phone, and it was about seven thirty. I slipped on my gold hoop earrings and my blue and gold heels, grabbed my phone and clutch, and headed out of the door. I slid in the car and started the engine, and before I drove off, I texted AJ that I was on my way and would see him there.

Adrian

I stood at my desk, getting ready to pack up and head home. I looked toward the door and saw my father talking to Hazel and handing her a stack of folders. *Aw shit. Let me hurry up and get out of here,* I thought to myself as I grabbed my phone and headed toward the door. I was almost out the door when I heard my dad call my name.

"Yes, sir?"

"Where are you going?" he asked as if it wasn't obvious. "Never mind that," he started before I could answer. "I need you to stay a few hours over to look over the Nemerson case, and I'm going to have Ms. Watson help you." My dad smiled and winked at me before walking out the door. I looked at my phone, and it was five o' clock. If I worked quick enough, I could meet up with Lina at eight with no problem.

I looked at Hazel, who I could tell was already exhausted. "You ready?"

"Yeah, let's do it."

We walked to one of the big worktables, spread the files out, and got to work. We were working on a money laundering case, and we had loads of information to sort through. Hazel sat across from me. Her blouse was slightly unbuttoned, and I could see the tops of her breast. My eyes traveled up her sexy neck and landed on her plump lips. Visions of me making out with her danced in my head. *Why does she have me like this?* I thought to myself, not knowing where these old feelings were coming from.

"Let's order some food," her soft voice broke my thoughts.

"Is Chinese cool?" I asked as I grabbed my phone.

"Yeah, that's cool."

I dialed up the local Chinese restaurant and ordered us some food. "It will be here shortly."

"Cool," she replied and continued to work.

"So, Hazel, how long have you been in town?" I asked.

"A few months. I was looking for work, and your dad must have come across my resume because his assistant called me and set up the interview." She sat back in the chair. "It looks like you are doing good for yourself. This is a nice firm, and I see from the corner office, you are the real MVP," she joked while eyeing my office.

"Yeah, I am the shit," I said as I popped my collar.

We worked a little more, and then I heard a buzz at the door. "That's the food." I got up and walked to the front to open the door. I grabbed the food and headed back. When I got there, Hazel was standing behind the receptionist's desk, messing with the switches. "What are you doing over there girl?" I asked as I started to bust open the food containers.

"Just trying to put on some music," she said as she plugged her phone up and hit a switch. The next thing I knew, nineties R&B flowed through the speakers.

"OK, I see you with the flashback Friday," I said as I nodded my head to a Blackstreet song and watched Hazel dance across the room. She was so sexy, swaying those hips and grooving with her hands over her head. I got up and started to dance as well. She danced over to me, and we started to dance together. She turned around and started to press herself against me, I grabbed her hips, and we swayed together for a little bit. The song went off, and we sat back down, laughing.

"You still got the moves, Ajie," she said, and I smiled because I had not heard that nickname in years.

"Yeah, I do a little something, something," I replied as I stuffed a spoonful of rice into my mouth.

"I didn't realize how much I missed you until just now," she added as she started to eat as well.

"Oh, word?" I replied with a smile. She nodded and smiled back. We sat there, eating, working, and just catching up and occasionally dancing to some songs that came over the speaker. I was having such a good time that I didn't even realize the time.

"Man, I'm getting tired, and I'm about to call it one," Hazel said as she walked over to her phone. "Oh my God, it's ten o'clock!" She shrieked, and I just knew I heard her wrong.

I looked at her and then grabbed my phone. Forty missed calls and thirty texts messages. *Fuck, Lina is going to fucking kill me,* I thought to myself as I called her phone, but I didn't get an answer. *Fuck!*

Lina

I pulled up to this little bar called The Den at exactly eight. I parked and scanned the parking lot for AJ's car, but I didn't see it. I pulled out my phone to call him, but I didn't get an answer. *He's probably on his way,* I thought to myself as I grabbed my purse and got out of the car. I walked inside and showed my ID to the security.

"Damn, lil' mama," he said as he took my ID. "You're looking real good." I smiled and thanked him and proceeded into the bar. As I walked through the crowd to find a spot at the bar counter, it felt like all eyes were on me, and instantly, I became really self-conscience.

Oh my God, do I look OK? How's my hair. Is this dress too short? Am I too big? I stopped those thoughts quickly and held my head up high as I strutted through. *Fuck that. I'm a sexy ass, thick ass, smart ass woman.* I smiled to myself and sat down at the bar.

"Hey, cutie. I'm Jo. What can I get you?" the bartender asked with a smile.

"Can I have a Long Island?"

"Coming right up," she said as she walked to her drink-making station.

I looked at my phone, and it was eight fifteen. I called AJ again, but still, no answer, so I left a voicemail. "Hey, bae, I'm here. Where are you?" I hung up and then thought to myself, *this nigga ain't gon' check that damn message.* I texted him, saying the same thing, then I opened snap to take some quick pictures of my fine ass.

"Let me help you out," Jo said, and I gave her my phone, stood up from the bar, and did a sexy pose. "Yes, bitch!" Jo geeked me up as I switched poses "Slay these hoes," she said, and I started laughing and sat back down to look and upload the pictures.

Damn, I look good. I put my phone down on the bar as Jo brought my drink. I took a sip, and I could definitely taste the liquor. "This is good," I said, and she smiled back.

"I had to make sure I made it as good as you look, girl." She flirted. "You are definitely killing the game in that dress!" She continued and now I was smiling, and I could feel my face blush a little.

"Thank you, boo," I replied as I took another sip of my drink.

"What brings you out tonight?" Jo asked as she made up another drink for another customer.

"Date night with my husband," I said as I looked at my phone again. Another fifteen minutes had rolled by. I called again. Again, no answer, so I sent another text. I finished my drink and asked Jo to bring me a shot of Don Julio. She brought the shot and some lime, and I threw it back and ordered a Tequila Sunrise. I called Adrian again but still didn't get an answer.

I sat at the bar, sipping on my fourth drink. My phone buzzed, and I grabbed it, hoping it was AJ with a good as explanation, but it wasn't. It was Ollie.

Ollie: Wassup trick how's the date going?

Me: It's not, Adrian never showed up

Ollie: Maybe he stuck in traffic

Me: Nigga its nine-thirty and his ass ain't answering the phone or text

I watched as the bubbles popped up indicating that Ollie was replying. I was waiting to see what he was going to say, but suddenly, it stopped. My phone buzzed again, but this time, it was a group chat.

Riley: Bitch ima kill that motherfucker

Sam: Girl is you ok

Ollie: No she ain't ok she been sitting at that bar all this time

Sam: Maybe it's a good explanation

Ollie: Yeah, maybe he's dead (coffin emoji)

Riley: Maybe Ima kill him (knife emoji)

The phone kept buzzing, so I put it on silent. I just didn't feel like it. *I'm pissed,* I thought to myself. *Fuck it though. I'm here, and if I gotta have fun, I'm going to do it myself. I'm too fucking cute to be sitting here looking like a lame.* "Jo, I need a shot," I slurred.

"No, you need to get out on that dancefloor and sweat the three shots you already had out."

"Say no more," I said as I stumbled off the barstool and started to groove on the dancefloor. The music flowed through me as I twirled and popped my hips. I held my phone up, snapping pictures and videos of me dancing. *I'm feeling myself,* I thought as I danced with my eyes closed. Next thing I knew, the liquor was taking control of me. I needed to sit down before the liquor sat me down. I was trying to make it back to the bar, but it must have been something wet on the floor, and suddenly, I was going down.

"Whoa, I got you, shorty," I heard a deep voice say as I felt a strong pair of hands on my waist. I turned around and saw the most beautiful smile. "You good?"

Jaxon Hudson

I walked into the bar with my guys. Today was a long day, and I just wanted to unwind and maybe rub on a big booty or two. As I made my way through the crowd, I spotted this fine woman dancing on the dancefloor. Her blue dress hugged her curvaceous body in such a way that you would have thought she was born with it. I started my way over to her. I figured now was the best time to shoot my shot and maybe get a little dance. As soon as I got to her, she started to walk off, and the next thing I knew, she was falling.

"Whoa, I got you, shorty," I said as I grabbed her by her waist to keep her from hitting the ground. "You good?" I asked as she turned around.

"Damn," we both said in unison. She was beautiful. She had these big, beautiful, dreamy eyes, a cute nose, and a nice set of full lips. She had long hair, and I could tell it was hers because it was frizzled from the heat. I smiled.

"I mean, uh," she stammered. "Thank you for not letting me fall. I think I might have had too much to drink." She laughed nervously.

"It's cool. That's what bars are for." I stared at her a little longer. *I think I know this woman,* I thought to myself, but I couldn't really place it. We stood there awkwardly for a moment. I could tell that I was losing her attention. "I'm Jaxon, Jaxon H—" She cut me off.

"Hud!" she exclaimed, and it threw me back a little because I hadn't heard that nickname since high school. "How have you been?" she asked.

"I'm sorry, but you kind of have me at a disadvantage. I'm not sure how we know each other," I said as we started to walk toward the bar.

"I mean, we really don't know each other. We went to the same high school. You were like a year behind me or something," she slurred. "I remember you because you played on the basketball team; everyone called you Hud." She laughed.

"What's funny?" I asked, clearly missing the joke.

"Nothing. It sounds cliché, but I kind of had a crush on you."

I looked at her and smiled. "Oh, really now? Wait, what did you say your name was?" She laughed.

"Oh, duh. I'm—" She was cut off by some guy.

"Darlina, I've been calling and texting you for the past thirty minutes. Let's go!" he said and then looked at me strangely before pulling her off the barstool.

"See you later, Jo!" she yelled to the bartender before disappearing into the crowd. I turned around on the stool and ordered a beer. *Darlina,* I thought to myself. *What a fine woman she was.* Jo handed me my drink, and I took a sip. I felt someone sit down next to me.

"Hey, wassup?"

"Wassup, man?" I replied without making eye contact.

"It's some fine hunnies in here tonight," he stated as he turned around to face the crowd and lit a cigar that he pulled from his jacket. He was an older guy and very well dressed to be in this hole in the wall.

"Shit, the finest one just got pulled out of here," I said as I turned around and stared at the crowd myself.

"Yeah, I can tell you a lot about that one." I looked at him.

"Do tell," I said, intrigued.

"Well," he started as he blew out smoke.

Darlina

"Damn it, Ollie!" I yelled, snatching my arm away.

"Girl bring your drunk ass on! Got us out here worried about you! Where is your phone!" he yelled as he grabbed me again and pulled me over to his car where Sam and Riley were waiting. They got out of the car, and I stared at all three of them as they talked all at once, scolding me for scaring them. The looks on their worried faces was somewhat hilarious, and I just couldn't help myself, and I burst into laughter.

"I know this bitch ain't," Ollie said with his face scrunched up.

"She's lit!" Riley said as she started laughing with me.

"Give me your keys, I'll take you home," Ollie said as he grabbed my clutch and pulled my keys out, popped the locks, and opened the front door. "Y'all follow me to her house, please. I know Adrian is losing his damn mind."

"Better his mind than his wife," I slurred as I opened the car door and climbed into the passenger seat. Ollie looked back at the other two.

"Whew, child, somebody is in their feelings," he said as he jumped in the front seat. Ollie started the engine and pulled out the parking lot. I turned up the radio and started to dance in my seat, yelling the lyrics out to the song as loud as I could. "I am too damn sober for this," he said as he turned the radio down a bit.

"You are no fun!" I yelled and turned the music back up. He looked at me and just laughed.

We pulled up to the house around eleven, and I said my goodbyes. I stumbled up to my front door, opened it, and quietly walked inside. It was dark, so I figured Adrian was sleep. I walked in the kitchen and tripped over the garbage can, which made a loud thud. I started laughing and then quickly shushed myself. *Get it together, girl, before you*—My thoughts were interrupted by the lights flicking on. I spun around quickly to see Adrian standing there in his wife beater and boxers.

"Hey, baby," I said loudly.

"Darlina, where have you been? I've been calling you all night." I laughed and walked over to him.

"No. I've been calling you all night," I said drunkenly as I pushed my finger against his forehead. He grabbed my arm. "Aw, we getting a little aggressive, are we?" I said as I pushed him against the counter and sexually pushed my body against his. "Why did you stand me up?" I asked aggressively as I grabbed his member and nibbled on his neck.

"Lina, you're drunk. Let's have this conversation in the morning."

Clearly, he isn't getting the message, I thought to myself as I started to suck on his neck and tug on his drawers.

"Lina, you're drunk," I mocked him. "Shut the fuck up and give me the dick," I said as I playfully smacked him in the face and pulled at his clothes. It seemed as if he was resisting, and it made me angry, so I got a little more aggressive.

"Stop!" he yelled and pushed me away. I tripped over my

heels and fell to the floor. I looked up at him in disbelief.

"Fuck you, Adrian! You've been acting brand new!" I yelled as I got up and stormed upstairs to our bedroom, slamming the door behind me.

Adrian

"Lina, you're drunk. Let's have this conversation in the morning," I said as she fumbled around my body, pulling at my clothes and getting aggressive. It was obvious that she had way too much to drink, and the smell of liquor on her breath was making me queasy. I knew she was trying to turn me on, but I was sober and tired, and all of this was just a turn off.

"Shut the fuck up and give me the dick," she slurred, and I was taken back by her aggressive language. It wasn't that I didn't like it. I just wasn't expecting it. Also, I was used to being in control, and right now, I was far from being in control. She smacked me, and I could tell she was playing, but it stung a bit. I tried to push her off as she pulled my clothes, but the more I tried to stop her, the harder she tried, and at this point, it wasn't playful sexy advances. She was really hitting me. I was now getting angry, and I yelled stop and pushed her away. She still had on her shoes and missed her step and landed right on her butt. She stared up at me in shock, but all I could think about was her beautiful breasts that had slipped out of her dress during the fall.

"Fuck you, Adrian! You've been acting brand new!" she screamed and ran upstairs, slamming the door to the bedroom.

"What the fuck!" I yelled more so at myself. I put my hands on my head and let out a deep sigh. *What the hell is going on with you, man? Why have you been treating her like this?* I thought to myself. "We are just different," I mumbled. *Different how though? What was different now?* I tried to search my brain, thinking of reasons as to why I could be acting like this, but I couldn't think of anything. *Shit just feels different.* "Is it me?" I asked myself. *It must be me,* I thought with a sigh. *Fuck it, Adrian. Get up there and apologize to your wife. You were in the wrong all day, and it's time to man up,* I thought to myself as I ran upstairs.

I walked into the room, ready to make amends, but I was too late. Lina was passed out in the bed, lying on her back with her feet dangling off the end and her arms sprawled above her head. Her hair was a mess, and her dress was raised up to her hips, and I could see her lacy underwear, and her breasts had once again slipped out. I could feel myself get hard as I stared at her. I walked over to the bed and pulled off her shoes and started to rub her thigh. She moved a bit. I crawled into the bed and started to kiss on her neck.

"Hey, babe. I'm sorry about today," I said as I started to kiss her lips.

"You're so mean to me, AJ," she said sleepily.

"I know, baby. I gotta work on that. Let me make it up to you," I said as I started to suck on her right breast and massage her left breast with my hand. Lina let out a soft moan. I moved my hand down her body and slid it into her panties. *Damn, she's wet as hell.* I sat up and positioned myself between her legs, pulled my stiff member out, and pushed her panties to the side. She let out a loud moan and arched her back as I slid inside of her. It had been a minute since we'd had sex, and she was very tight. I groaned in pleasure as her love box gripped and soaked me.

Aw shit, Hazel... No. Lina. I couldn't help but think about Hazel and how her shirt was slightly unbuttoned. I grabbed Lina by her hips and dragged her further down the bed so I could stand up. "You trying to be a tease, huh? With your breast all out and shit!" I yelled as I thrust harder. Her euphoric moans filled the air. The deeper I plunged, the more slippery her slope became. I started to think about Hazel again. I thought about her swaying hips when she was dancing,

"Turn around," I growled as I flipped her over. "Come on. Get on them knees." I yanked her up and started to hit it from the back real good. Visions of Hazel pressing up against me when we were dancing filled my head. I could still smell the scent of her hair. "Yeah, you wanna dance and shit, right? You wanna be a little freaky tease, right?" I groaned as I grabbed Lina by her hair, yanking her head back and pounding her dripping pussy.

"Ow, Adrian, you're hurting me," she groaned in both pleasure and pain.

"Ow, you're hurting me," I mocked her. "Shut the fuck up and take this dick," I said as I pushed her head into the mattress. It must have turned her on because her body exploded in ecstasy. She screamed my name, but it was muffled because I was still pushing down on her head. Both visions of Lina and Hazel clouded my mind, and I could feel myself about to nut. *Aw shit, I'm about to explode* "Fucckkkkk!" I moaned as I emptied myself inside of her.

Lina fell completely to the bed, and I stumbled back weakly, and both of our exhausted pants filled the air.

Chapter Two

Lina (Saturday)

I woke up with a pounding headache. I looked over at the clock. *Three in the morning.* I looked on the opposite side of me, Adrian was laying there, sleeping. I tried to get up, but my body felt like I had been hit by an eighteen-wheeler. I finally pulled myself out of the bed and started to make my way toward the bathroom. My dress was bunched up around my waist, and the chain that was around the neckline was broken. I could hear it scraping against the floor as I walked into the bathroom.

The floor was cold, and I caught a slight chill as I turned on the light. I stood in front of the mirror and stared at myself. My makeup was smeared all over my face, and the front of my dress was hanging down, exposing my breast. I slid my dress off and looked at my sides. They were covered in big, red bruises. *What the fuck, man?* I thought as I walked over and sat on the toilet. *Damn, even my coochie is sore as hell.* I stood up, wiped, and washed my hands.

I looked at my body one more time and then walked back into the room. I stood in the middle of the floor, staring at AJ as he slept in the bed. *He has never had sex with me like that before. Shit, if I didn't know any better, I would have thought he was fucking someone else.* I shook that thought out of my head and grabbed my night clothes out of the drawer. Slipping them on, I walked downstairs and into the kitchen. I grabbed the Tylenol out of the cabinet and opened the refrigerator to grab a water bottle. I plopped on the couch in the living room and took the medicine.

Reaching for the remote control, I saw AJ's phone out of the corner of my eye. *Don't even think about it Lina.* I thought to myself as I grabbed the remote control and turned on the TV. *Yeah, but he was just up there fucking you like you was some new pussy though.* My mind wandered back and forth. *Yeah, on one hand, I was looking good as hell last night, but on the other hand, I'm bruised up.* My mind continued to wander, but I was too tired to follow it. I contemplated on whether or not I should go back upstairs, but for some reason, I felt awkward, laying with him. I laid down on the couch and scrolled through Netflix until I found something suitable to fall asleep to. I laid there, watching the opening credits, and then I drifted off to sleep.

I woke up and looked around. I was still on the couch, and the TV was on, but the screen was asking if I was still watching. I stood up, rubbed my eyes, and walked upstairs into the bedroom. *What the hell?* I thought to myself as I looked around. Adrian was gone, and the bed was made. "Adrian?" I called out but got no response. I looked at the clock, and it was just turning ten. *Where in the hell could he be this early on a Saturday?* I walked back downstairs and noticed a note on the refrigerator.

Hey Lina, had to run to the office, be back shortly. Also, I left you some breakfast inside. Adrian

I opened the refrigerator and saw the magic bullet, filled

with veggies and fruit, ready to be made into a smoothie on the top shelf. "Ugh!" I yelled out in frustration and slammed the door. Quickly running upstairs, I changed into some yoga pants and a T-shirt. I brushed my teeth, washed my face, pulled my hair into a ponytail, and then tossed on an old Nike cap. I walked downstairs and grabbed my things and left out the house. Hopping into the car, I headed to this little diner around the corner. I walked in, sat at a booth, grabbed the menu, and waited for the waitress to come.

"Hey, good morning. I'm Mia, and I'll be your waitress today. Can I start you off with something to drink?"

I looked up. "Hey, yeah. Can I have a coffee to start?" I said while glancing at the menu. "And a veggie omelet with hash browns. Cheese on both." I continued, and she wrote it on her pad.

"OK, I'll put that in and will be back shortly with your coffee."

I smiled, and she walked off. I looked at my phone and started to replay my videos from last night. I couldn't help but laugh at my twisted face.

"Oh my God, I was so drunk!" I skipped through the videos and then switched over to Facebook. The waitress brought my coffee, cream, and sugar. The strong smell of coffee beans hit my nose as I reached for the cream. I heard the bell to the diner door ring, indicating that someone was coming in. I glanced up from my cup for a moment, and there he was—the guy from last night. He caught my glance, I quickly looked down and started to open packs of cream.

"Hey," he said as he sat down at the table. "It must be fate, seeing you back to back like this," he said as the waitress walked up with my plate of food.

"Thank you," I said, as Jaxon started to order his food. I sat, a little confused. *Why was he sitting here and about to have breakfast with me, and why was he so damn fine?* I stared at him, admiring his smooth, chocolate skin. I watched his lips as he ordered his food. *Damn, I bet they are soft and sweet.* Thoughts ran through my head as I forced myself to not lick my lips. He caught me looking and smiled. I had never seen teeth so white. He had a sexy beard, and his hair was braided up into one of those fuckboy buns, like the rapper's wear. I quickly glanced down and began to season my eggs. The waitress walked off and I could feel his eyes on me. My body started to heat up, and at that moment I wished I would have ordered the iced tea.

"So, do you see something you like?" he asked, and his deep voice was like a sweet song in my ear.

"Excuse me?" I said as I started to eat.

"I mean, I see you drooling all over me and everything." He smiled, and I glanced up.

"Whatever," I laughed and mixed my food around.

The waitress came back with water and asked me how my food was, and then she walked away again.

"Was that your husband that pulled you away last night?" he asked, while opening his straw and sipping on his water.

"Naw, my husband stood me up. That was my best friend,

43

Ollie," I said as I stuffed a forkful of hash browns into my mouth.

"Oliver Phillips. I knew he looked familiar," he said as he stared at me. "Why can't I remember you?" He questioned and I laughed.

"Because I was a nerd in high school, and you were a jock." I joked while sipping on my coffee.

"Yeah, but I wasn't a shallow jock," he said as the waitress came back to the table with his food.

"You guys need anything?" she asked, and we both shook our heads no.

"Didn't you use to wear like cornrows in your hair and like glasses and braces and shit like that?"

"Yeah, that was me. Those were definitely my fugly years," I said as I sipped on my coffee.

"Well, thank God for growth," he said as he held his glass up in a cheers motion.

"Yes, thank God for growth," I repeated and clinked my mug against his glass.

Adrian

I woke up and glanced at the clock. It was eight in the morning. I looked toward the bathroom door to see if it was closed, and it wasn't. *Where is this girl at?* I asked myself as I got out of bed and walked downstairs. I saw her lying on the couch as one of her shows played in the background. I stared at her as she lay in her favorite plaid pajamas. They used to be really loose on her, but now they fit very snug. *How is she gaining this weight?* I thought to myself as I walked in the kitchen and started to make her a breakfast smoothie. I was going to make sure she got back to the size she was when I met her. As I was preparing the smoothie, I heard my phone go off. I walked over to it and opened the text message from an unknown number

> *Unknown number: Hey it's Hazel, can we meet up*
>
> *Me: Sure, just text me where.*

I walked back into the kitchen and put the pre-made smoothie into the fridge and then went upstairs and brushed my teeth. *Is it weird that I would rather spend my morning with someone else other than my wife? I mean, I wouldn't even be interested with someone else if she would just be the way I want her to be. Just stay slim, keep that silky hair in, and stop hanging around those ratchet ass friends of hers. I mean, being married into the Long family is a damn privilege, and I feel like she's wasting it.* I could feel myself getting upset. A year ago, I didn't see my life like this. *I'm unhappy with the way things are right now, and I owe it to myself to get out and get some fresh ass—er, um air.* I laughed at myself as I walked back into the room and changed my clothes. *I'm not going to cheat on my wife, but there isn't a rule that says I can't have a good time with other women while being married.* I looked in the mirror again and then walked down the stairs. I left Lina a note and headed out of the house.

Jaxon

I pulled into the parking lot of a little diner. I had a damn headache from being out all night, and all I wanted was a damn breakfast sampler. I had taken home a little dip from the bar, but she was whack as hell. I stepped out of my car and walked into the diner. I searched for the seat, and boom, there was the little shorty from last night. I caught her glance and walked over and sat with her.

"Hey, it must be fate, seeing you back to back like this." I slid into the booth seat across from her. The waitress brought a plate of food to the table and started to take my order. "Let me get, uh, the breakfast sampler. Eggs scrambled with cheese and onion, hash browns also with cheese and onions. Bacon, sausage, and ham, and the pancakes." As I was ordering my food, I caught Lina staring me down. I flashed her a quick smile before going over the order with the waitress.

"I'll put that right in," she said and walked away.

"So, do you see something you like?" I asked jokingly and she laughed. Watching her as she spoke, I couldn't help noticing how beautiful she was. She had a smile that could light up the darkest nights. Her eyes were warming and the naturalness of her was steady pulling me in. *I need to make shorty mine, but damn, she's married*. I looked at her ring as she was talking to the waitress. "Was that your husband that pulled you away last night?"

47

I asked after the waitress walked away.

"Naw, my husband stood me up. That was my best friend, Ollie."

I remember Ollie; he was very popular in high school, but why couldn't I remember her? I studied her face as she ate and talked, and then it hit me.

"Didn't you use to wear like cornrows in your hair and like glasses and braces and shit like that?" I asked as I started to season my eggs and mix my food together. She joked about being fugly, but right now, she was nothing less than gorgeous. "Well, thank God for growth," I said as I held my glass up in a cheers motion.

"Yes, thank God for growth," she repeated and clinked her glass against mine.

I laughed. "Aye, you're real as hell, Shorty."

The waitress came back, and I asked for the check. She cleared the table and walked away. "Here," Lina said as she started to go into her purse.

"Woman, do not insult me like that." She looked at me and then put her purse down.

"Well, OK, big man, you got it." She laughed, and I smiled. The waitress came back, and I paid the bill and left the tip. I stood up.

Standing up, I decided it was now or never. "Hey, do you wanna get out of here and do something?" I asked in a hopeful tone, but the look on her face was already a shut down.

"I mean, this was fun and everything, but I got a hair

appointment in like an hour." I looked at her to see if she was serious.

"A hair appointment? For real? You ain't gotta lie, Craig," I said to her in disbelief. She stood up. *Damn, shorty got body.* I stared at her thick thighs in those yoga pants. *Somebody been eating their beans and cabbage,* I thought as I followed her out the diner and into the parking lot.

"Look at this," she said as she quickly pulled her hat off, exposing a messy ponytail. "I need a hair miracle." I laughed, and she put her hat back on.

"So, what, you about to get a press and curl or some shit? I can wait around for that," I said, hoping to get some more time with her.

"Naw fam. I'm getting a full blown sew in." She laughed.

"Why?" I asked while pulling on her ponytail. I could tell my reaction shocked her by the way her eyes bucked. "I mean, you got all that pretty ass hair, and you are just going to hide it for some fake shit?" She grew quiet. "My bad, shorty. I didn't mean to offend you."

"Naw, it's not that," she started but then stopped. I could tell she was trying to search for the right words. "My husband just prefers me with long, silky hair." She looked away, and I could tell she was kind of ashamed.

"Well, he's an idiot—" I stopped myself, and there was an awkward silence. She opened her car door and got in. I grabbed the door before she could close it. "Can I see you again?" I asked in a hopeful manner.

"Jaxon, I'm married." She pulled the door closed and rolled down the window.

"That's cool, shorty. I understand. I will just sulk and drink all my sorrows away at the bar tonight," I joked, and she smiled.

"It was nice catching up with you," was the last thing she said as she pulled out of the parking lot.

Hazel Watson

I laid in the bed, thinking about the night before. Adrian was still fine as hell with that damn muscular body, clean shaved face, that nice ass BMW, and all that family money. I mean, yes, I had my own family money, but damn, there ain't nothing like a man's money. I couldn't believe he married that Darlina chick. I mean, like really, what the fuck type of name was DaRLinA? I laughed to myself as I thought about that SpongeBob meme that'd been floating around the internet. I was about to get out of bed when I heard my phone receive a text message.

Unknown number: Hey how is it going?

Me: Slow, but it's going

Unknown number: I'm counting on you to get it done

Me: Believe me I will.

I got out of bed, walked into the bathroom, and turned on the shower. Walking back into my room, I grabbed my phone.

Me: Hey it's Hazel, can we meet up

Adrian: Sure, just text me where

I texted him my address and then went back into the bathroom to jump in the shower. I wanted to get nice and fresh just in case he let me sit on his face. I washed my hair and body, got out and pulled on my silk robe. I sat on the couch and patiently waited. About ten minutes later, I heard the doorbell ring. I ran in the bathroom, turned on the sink, and splashed water on my face, chest, and hair. I pulled my robe open a little and then walked to the front and opened the door.

"Hey, sorry. I was in the shower," I said seductively as I let him in.

"No problem," Adrian said as he followed me in. I made sure to put a twist in my hip as I led him in. I could feel the heat from his eyes all over my body.

"Here. Sit down. I was just about to pour me up a drink. You want something?" I asked as I pulled a bottle of Hennessy and started to pour a shot.

"It's nine in the morning but fuck it. Do me one," he said as he sat on the couch. *I can do you one, all right.* I laughed at the thought and poured him a shot as well.

"So how was your night?" I asked as I handed him his glass and sat next to him, letting my robe slip open a little more.

"Shit, it was cool. I just chilled." He took the shot, grabbed the bottle, and poured up another.

"You seem stressed. What's going on?" I asked as I took my shot and poured up another one.

"It's nothing," he said, but I didn't believe him. I poured up two more shots, and we took them together. "So wassup, Hazel? What am I doing over here?"

"Well, I just enjoyed spending time with you last night. I wanted a little more," I said as I got up and walked behind the couch where he was sitting. "But you sound so stressed. I think *you* need a little more," I said as I started to rub his shoulders.

"Yeah," he moaned out. "I do need the attention."

"You ain't getting any attention at home from your little

wife?" I mocked.

"Little wife? That's funny. Lately, I feel like I'm living with a different person," he said in a dispassionate tone.

"What you mean, baby?" I asked as I deeply massaged his shoulders.

"She's just not the woman I married; she's gaining weight, trying to do that nappy ass natural shit, always with these ratchet ass friends, and I feel like she's not trying to fit into the normal way of my family. She doesn't even want to spend time at the country club with my family on the weekend." He paused. "Do I sound crazy?"

I laughed. "No, you just sound like a man that knows what he wants and what he's not getting."

"I'm glad you understand," he said as he took another shot.

"You're gonna be fucked up, boy."

"Shit, right now, this is the only thing that's keeping me from losing my shit."

I stopped rubbing his shoulders and came around to sit next to him.

"Let me help you take some stress off," I said as I reached over to rub in between his legs.

"Shit, in the words of Drake, *show me a good time*," he said as he took another shot, this time out of the bottle. I smiled, got on my knees in front of him, and unbuckled his pants. I pulled out his already hard staff and wrapped my mouth around it. He let out a soft moan as I bobbed my head up and down.

"Open that robe and let me see them titties," he said as he pulled my robe. I undid the strap and let my breasts hang as I slurped faster. "Shit," he groaned, which turned me on. I grabbed his dick and started to jerk it off as I hit him with the triple gwack-gwack slurp. "Fuck, Hazel," he moaned as he grabbed a handful of my hair and pushed my head down until I gagged. *Thank God my gag reflex is long gone.* I choked and gagged on his dick until tears ran down my face.

"Spit on my shit, bitch," he growled, and I did what I was told. *My old money and his old money finna rule the world. He's gonna leave his fat wife, and I'm going to be living the Long dream with my feet kicked up.* Just the thought of being Mrs. Long turned me on, and the next thing I knew, I was going ham on his ass. I was literally trying to vacuum suck his shit into my trachea.

"Aw shit!" he yelled as he held my head, and the next thing I knew, I was feeling his warm cream all in my throat. I kept sucking until he was completely empty. I swallowed, and he let out a weak moan as I let his limp dick fall out of my mouth. "Damn, girl," he said with a last breath before he closed his eyes.

Adrian

I woke up in a fuzzy daze. *Where am I?* was all I could think as I looked around. *Oh yeah, I'm at Hazel's place. I guess I dozed off.* "Hazel," I called out as I stood and buttoned up my pants.

"Hey, sleepy head," she said as she came out a room fully dressed.

"How long was I out?" I asked, searching for my phone. "A few hours," she replied nonchalantly. *Did this bitch just say hours? Hold the fuck up.* I finally found my phone in the crevice of the couch. I looked at the time, and it was going on two.

"Damn, girl, why you let me sleep this long? I told Lina I would be back."

"Boy, I ain't worried about what you told your bitch." I looked at her like she was crazy.

"That's my wife, so don't disrespect her."

She stared me down and started to laugh. "Nigga, your dick was just in my throat. We are way past disrespect." Her snotty ass tone turned me off.

"Ight," I said as I grabbed my shit and left out. *What the fuck did I just do? Did I really just let this girl top me off?* I thought to myself as the visions of Hazel's head in my lap ran around carelessly in my head. *I mean, damn, that shit was off the fucking chain, but that shit was not supposed to go down like that, and I damn sure wasn't supposed to be there for five fucking hours.* I couldn't just go home smelling like liquor with no explanation, so I decided to call Aaron.

"Yo, wassup, bro!" he answered on the first ring.

"Yo, nigga, you at the crib? I need some advice."

"Slide through. I'm here."

"Ight, I'll be there in like fifteen," I said and hung up the phone. I pulled up to the Aaron's crib, got out, and rang the doorbell.

"It's open!" he yelled from inside. I opened the door and walked in. Aaron was in the kitchen, making a sandwich. "Wassup, nigga? You want one?" he asked as he folded the thinly sliced meat on the bread.

"Naw, I'm good, bro, but thanks," I said as I sat on the bar stool and leaned on the counter. He looked at me.

"Wassup, man? You seem like you got a lot on your plate or something?" I could hear the concern in his voice.

"Man, I did something really dumb," I replied, not really wanting to admit it.

"What you do? Cheat on Lina or something?" He asked with a laugh as he placed a slice to lettuce on his sandwich. I sat quietly, wondering how in the hell he guessed it. He looked up from his sandwich and caught my gaze. "Naw, nigga, tell me you didn't?" he asked in disbelief. I still didn't say anything. I just didn't want to admit it. "With who?" he asked as he started to eat.

"Hazel," I shamefully admitted.

"Nigga!" he said, throwing his sandwich down on the plate and standing in aghast. We both sat in silence for what seemed like hours. "How did this happen?" he asked with an apprehensive tone.

I started to explain how Lina and I weren't connecting and how she was changing and that I'd been giving her a hard time. I told him about last night and how I was with Hazel and stood Lina up. I also told him how I was with Lina but really thinking about Hazel and then finally the main part, which was Hazel sucking me off. He sat there with his mouth open, and he stared in disbelief.

"Nigga," he finally said as he shook his head. "This entire situation has me perplexed." He paused and then shook his head again. "First of all, Lina is a good ass woman, and the fact that you are shaming her about her body is wrong as hell," he started. I tried to protest, but he cut me off. "Naw, bro, I'm your friend, and you need to hear this shit," he continued. "Now, I know you and Hazel had a thing back in the day, but just because she's back in your presence doesn't mean you should just throw away an entire marriage. Especially not over some extra pounds and a hairstyle. And if that was your excuse for standing Lina up and then leaving her sleep to go over another bitch house, then, bro…" He paused, and I could tell he was contemplating. "You're stupid as hell." he said, shaking his head. He grabbed his sandwich and started eating, and I sat there in my feelings.

Finally, I stood up. "Man, fuck you, Aaron," I said in anger.

He laughed, "Nigga, don't get mad at me because you fucked up. You came over here because you knew I was gonna be real with you." I looked at him as he grinned.

"Motherfucker, why are you grinning like this shit is a joke or something?" I asked, getting more upset.

"Bro, it is a joke," he said as he took another bite of his sandwich. "You just told me you cheated on Lina because she got a little thicker. And you cheated on her with Hazel, really? Hazel is damn near built like a boy. It really sounds like the beginning of a bad joke." He laughed again and took another bite of his sandwich. He was pissing me off, and my blood was starting to boil.

"Man, fuck you," I said as I smacked the sandwich right out of his hands. He looked at me, looked at the sandwich and then back at me.

"Damn, man, don't fuck up my shit 'cause you fucking up your shit," he said as I stormed out the kitchen. "So, you not gonna clean this up!" he yelled behind me as I slammed the front door and got in my car.

I can't believe him. The nerve of that motherfucker, I thought as I started the car and drove back to my house. *He doesn't get it. How am I stupid for being unhappy?* I looked at the clock, and it was five. *What the fucccckkkkk? Where is the day going?* I pulled into the nearest liquor store to grab a bottle of Henny to help me level out. I cracked it open, took a swig, and headed home.

Aaron

I cleaned up the mess that AJ left on the kitchen floor. I can't believe he spazzed out on me like that. Shit, I was just trying to be real with his ass. He knows he is in the fucking wrong, and that's why he got so upset. I mean, yes, Lina has gained a little weight, but it's happy marriage weight. *Shit, it actually made her ass look better,* I thought as I remembered how she looked the last weekend I'd seen her. That ass was growing, and those hips were showing, and this goofy was falling all over Hazel again. I mean, Hazel has a cute ass face, but she's built like a boy, all athletic and shit. I know that was his boo in college, but she did him dirty, and then he stole Lina from me. I mean, I wasn't dating her, but he knew I liked her. *But of course, he had to go swinging his dick around and shit.* I sat at the table and thought about it some more. *You know what? Fuck it. Let him fuck Hazel. That way, I can come up with the layup and show Lina how a real nigga supposed to act.* I pulled out my phone and texted Adrian.

Me: You know what bro, I was tripping. I sat here and thought about it. If you are really unhappy with Lina then you gotta do what's best to make you happy, and if that's doing Hazel, then do her. You only got one life to live bro, you gotta live it.

Adrian: Hell yeah, you get it.

I laughed. This nigga always just needed one motherfucker to agree with his stupidity to make it make sense. *I'll be that nigga if it means I can have Lina.*

Lina

I stood in the mirror, looking at my new hairstyle. I decided against the sew in and went for some box braids. I had the top pulled up into a bun and the back down. *Damn, girl, you look good.* I pulled my sundress tightly around my booty and started twerking in the mirror. "Ayyy, ayyy, ayyy, make that booty jump!" I sang my own little tune as I got lower and lower. *That motherfucker fucked me so good last night; my booty getting bigger.* I laughed and walked back into the kitchen to start on dinner. It was about five, and I had been at the hairdresser all damn day, but it was definitely worth it.

I walked into the kitchen and over to the counter. I had already battered the chicken wings and started the grease; all that was left was to fry the chicken up. I placed a few pieces in the fryer and dropped the basket into the bubbling grease. Walking to the stove, I turned off the rice, corn, and peas mixture. I added some butter and sprinkled in some salt and pepper and then walked back over to the counter.

"Whew," I said as I grabbed my wine glass and took a sip of my favorite sweet Moscato.

Damn, that dick he put on me last night was amazing; I mean, he legit beat this pussy up. I mean, I can't remember much, but I do remember busting some good ass nuts. I could feel myself getting hot, just thinking about it. I took another sip of my wine, placed it back on the counter, and went to check on the chicken. It was frying really good and smelling delicious. The timer went off just as I got to it. Pulling the basket up and shaking the grease off, I dumped the golden-brown wings onto a paper-towel-layered plate. I covered them with foil and added more chicken to the fryer.

"Shit," I said as the smell of baked bread filled the air. "I almost forgot." I continued as I walked to the oven to check on the biscuits. They were done, so I pulled them out and buttered them up. I sipped on my glass until the timer on the fryer went off again. I pulled the chicken out, turned off the fryer and admired my masterpiece. *Dinner is done.*

I walked to the TV, turned it on, and hit the Pandora app to play some music. I wanted the mood to be perfect. Adrian and I had been butting heads, but I love that man to death. *That's my husband and we are in this shit forever.* I thought as everything that happened these last few days flashed in my head. At the end of the day I am his wife, and even though we fight, I know he loves me, and I love him.

"That is all that matters," I said to myself as I walked back into the kitchen, grabbed my wine. And started dancing to the sexy slow jams.

Suddenly, the front door swung open, and Adrian walked awkwardly into the house.

"Hey, babe," I said, staring at the half-empty bottle of Hennessey in his hand. "Are you pregaming for something?"

"What the fuck is that goofy ass shit on your head?" he slurred and drank more from the bottle. "I fucking thought we both agreed that you were going to get that long shit back." He snarled and I looked at him like he was crazy, but he was right. I did say I was going to get the weave.

"I thought you would like this, Adrian," I said with disappointment.

"Well, next time, don't fucking think, and just do what the hell you are told," he scolded as he took another swig of the bottle.

"I'm sorry. You're right. I'll take it down tomorrow if that makes you happy," I said as I walked into the living room to turn the music down. *Mood ruined.* "I don't want to argue, because you are drunk. Let's just eat dinner," I said as I walked back into the kitchen and started to fix the plates.

"That looks good, but what are you eating?" He asked in a condescending tone

Here we fucking go. "What the fuck you mean? I just slaved over this stove, and I'm going to enjoy this dinner," I said as I took a big bite of the chicken wing. *Damn, I really outdid myself with this seasoning.*

"You are fat, and you fucking disgust me," he spat out as he knocked my plate out of my hand. "I've been trying to be nice to you, give you subtle hints, but you refuse to take them. I am no longer attracted to you, because you let yourself get big and fucking sloppy! I mean, look at your fucking breast and how they are hanging out your dress like you are some fucking Amber Rose video slut or something. And that fucking natural hair, black power shit, I just can't take it anymore. If you can't fucking fit into the normality of the Long family, then maybe you ain't fucking Long material!" he growled out.

I stood there, speechless. My whole body was numb, and I felt a sharp pain in my chest. I could feel my heartbreaking. I gasped for air as I fought back the tears. *Lina, do not let this trifling ass nigga see you crying.* He stared at me with glassy eyes and then finished the bottle. I was so offended that I couldn't even talk. I just grabbed my phone, keys, and purse and left out of the house.

Jaxon

I walked into the bar around nine. The music was loud, but it was pretty empty. I sat on the stool. "Hey, Jo, let me get a beer?" I asked the bartender. She grabbed the beer and then leaned closer to me.

"You need to check on your girl," she said as she nodded her head toward the end of the bar. I glanced down and saw Lina sitting there with her head laying on the bar. She had a half of bottle of tequila in one hand and a glass in the other. I looked back at Jo.

"What's going on with her?"

"I don't know. It has something to do with her husband. She's been here for over an hour, and she's really messed up." I looked back down the bar, and Lina was taking another shot, this time out of the bottle.

"I'll handle it," I said as I got up and walked down to the other end of the bar. "Excuse me, miss. Don't you think you are too pretty to be drinking like that?" I joked, trying to lighten the mood.

"First of fucking all—" She started but then stopped when she realized it was me. "Hud!" she yelled. "I didn't know you would be here. I am so happy to see you," she slurred.

"I'm glad you were able to make it. I just didn't know you would be so spirited," I said as I grabbed the bottle out of her hand

"No, don't. I need that. I am so stressed and depressed…" She paused. "Stressed and depressed; I made a rhyme," she said as she started laughing, and then she stopped. "He hates me. All I wanted to do was be a good wife, but I failed, and now he hates me," she said as she drank the little bit of liquor left out of her glass.

"What happened?" I asked concerningly. She looked at me and started to cry hysterically. She tried to explain the situation, but I couldn't understand. It all sounded like gibberish through the tears and liquor. "Whoa, whoa, whoa. Shorty, you gotta calm down..." I paused and looked around at the few people that were staring. "Jo, can I get some water!" I yelled over the music, and she nodded and brought over a bottle. "Come on. We are going outside to get some fresh air," I said as I pulled her through the small crowd and out the door. We walked over to my car, and I handed her the water bottle. "Here. Drink this," I said as I twisted open the cap and gave her the bottle. She started to drink it really fast, and then she started to gag.

"I think I'm about to—" She stopped talking and instantly started to throw up on the side of the car. I held back her hair as she finished up.

"You OK?" I asked as she stood up and wiped her mouth with the back of her hand.

"Yeah." She put some more water in her mouth, swished it around, and then spat it out. "Thank you. I almost lost it back there," she said as she drank the rest of the bottle.

"So, are you going to tell me why you were staring at the bottom of the bottle?"

"Just marital problems," she said, but I could hear the sorrow in her voice.

"Get in and let's talk," I said as I walked over to the passenger side and opened the door. She got in. I closed the door and walked around to the driver side. "So?" I inquired as I got in and closed the door.

We sat in silence for what seemed like an hour. I didn't want to pressure her. "You know you are looking fine as fuck in those braids." She looked at me and smiled. "I mean, damn, girl, that shit is all you."

"Stop playing," she said with a giggle.

"That smile gets me, girl," I flirted.

"Stop before I start blushing," she said, and I stared at her. *Damn, she's beautiful. Those eyes and them lips—oh my God.* "Shit has been real crazy the last few weeks, and this weekend just really took the cake." She started to tell me about everything, starting from yesterday morning all the way down until the last few hours, and the last words he said to her even hurt my damn feelings. "And I just don't get it. I've tried my hardest to be the best wife to him, coming home from work, cooking and cleaning. I mean, damn, I'm losing myself in the process. I'm damn near starving myself to lost weight to fit his image. My edges are thinning from the constant sew ins. I mean, damn, I have to tip toe around his feelings all the time because oh no, Adrian can do no fucking wrong, but every week, he's arguing with me about dumb shit. He abuses me mentally and emotionally, and I take it with a smile on my face." I could hear the anger in her voice.

"But why do you just take the abuse?" I asked, trying to get a better understanding.

She looked at me with the most serious face. "Because I'm his wife, and I have to be pleasant."

I stared at her. "What the hell does that mean?" I asked uncertainly.

"I have to be nice because he is my husband. At the end of the day, I am here to be his peace..." She paused. "But who is going to be my peace?" she asked, and I could hear the heartache in her voice as she wept silently to herself. I sat there, wishing that I could just hold her, but I didn't know if that was appropriate, and I didn't want her to think I was making a move on her.

"Lina, listen," I started, trying to figure out what to say. "Yes, that is your husband, but you only have one life to live, shorty, and at the end of the day, you gotta be nice for what to that nigga? I mean, shit, a marriage is fifty-fifty, and you sitting here taking his abuse for what? His ass damn sure ain't being nice to you, so fuck being nice to him. A real man doesn't body shame and belittle the woman he loves." I looked at her as she stared forward.

"I feel you, but who am I without him?" Her doubtful tone angered me, but I wasn't mad at her. I was pissed at the damage this nigga was doing to her.

"A beautiful, strong, and intelligent woman."

"What?" she asked, uncertain.

"That's who you are without him. I mean, look. You have a degree, right?"

"Yeah."

"You make your own money, drive your own car. You do not have to be held down by a nigga that ain't even down for you…" I paused, waiting to hear a response, but she sat quietly. "Plus, shorty, you are fine as hell, girl. That body of yours is banging, and the way that natural hair flow when you dance…" I thought back to last night when I first saw her in the bar.

"You look good, girl. You see I had to add you on snap."

She laughed. "Yeah, your bitmoji looks just like you."

I laughed too. "That's what I'm talking about. Smile, girl. You're beautiful," I said as I pulled the sun visor down and opened the mirror. "Look at you. That's a real one in your reflection. Ain't no point in being nice to a nigga that can't appreciate that beautiful face." She smiled again as she looked at her reflection.

"I do look good, don't I?" she asked as she changed her angles in the mirror.

"Better than a large plate of fried chicken and rice," I joked, and she quickly looked at me and then started laughing.

"You're real funny."

"I know…" I paused. "You know what? Let's get out of here," I said as I started the engine up.

"What about my car?" she asked, concerned.

"It will be here when we get back," I said as I pulled out of the parking lot.

Chapter Three

Adrian (Sunday)

I woke up hot and sweaty. I looked around, and I was lying face first on the couch. Visions from the last few hours danced in my head. *Then maybe you ain't fucking Long material!* I thought I wanted to hurt her with those words until I saw the pain flood deep in her eyes. And when she grabbed her chest, I knew I had broken her heart. I thought back to the things I said, and I really didn't mean them. I just said them out of drunken spite.

Damn, Adrian, what the fuck is wrong with you? I hit myself in the head as I walked into the kitchen to clean up the plate of food that I knocked out of Lina's hand. *I was really fucking tripping, man. I can't believe the liquor had me acting out of my body like that.* I finished cleaning up and then put me some food on the plate and placed it in the microwave. Once it was heating up, I walked over to the phone to check the time. *Damn, it's three in the morning.* I looked outside, and Lina's car wasn't in the driveway. *I'm sure she is probably at one of her friend's house, cooling off.* I thought to myself as I grabbed my phone. I will definitely make it up to her tomorrow, but until then, Ima text Hazel and see if I can shove my dick down her throat.

I texted her, and to my surprise, she answered. I sent her the address and then went into the kitchen to eat. *Damn, this shit is good as hell.*

Lina

I moaned as my body was sent into pure ecstasy. "OK, Jaxon." I giggled as he massaged my feet with warm coconut oil.

"Your mouth is saying OK, but your body is still tensed, and before I lay down, I want to make sure you are completely relaxed," he said as he massaged up and down my leg.

"I am relaxed. I mean, damn, you've fed me and massaged my entire body. I'm good," I said as I slid my leg out of his grip. I grabbed my phone, and it was going on 3:30 a.m.

Damn, time sure does fly when you are having a good time. We'd been taking shots, singing along to songs and dancing. We went joy riding and got some greasy ass comfort food, and now we were here at his crib, and he'd just given me the most sensual massage I'd ever had. I couldn't even remember the last time Adrian touched me like this, and I knew I shouldn't have been here, putting myself in this position, but it felt good to be catered to, even if it was just for a night. And shit, Jaxon's ass was so damn fine. I mean, he had that bad fuckboy look, like he was the type of nigga to fuck you dry and then eat all your baby's fruit snacks.

"You OK?" he asked, breaking me out of my thoughts.

"Yeah, I'm good. Just thinking."

"Well, it looks like you were thinking of a way to get me out of my clothes," he joked, and I laughed. He laughed too. "Naw, but for real, lil' momma, I'm exhausted, and I can tell you are too. How about we just lay back on these couches and Netflix and chill until we fall asleep?" I looked at him, and I could tell he was not trying to fuck me. I laid with him on the couch as he scrolled through the movies, finally settling on some action movie. I didn't even make it through the opening credits.

Damn, something smells good. I woke up to the smell of eggs and bacon. I was still lying on the couch but alone. I could hear pots and pans banging in the kitchen, so I knew Jaxon must have been in there, making some good ol' breakfast. I reached for my phone. It was noon, and I didn't have any missed calls. *Damn, so I've been gone all night, and this nigga ain't even tried to hit me up? Fuck him,* I thought as I threw my phone on the table and sat up.

"Hey. Good afternoon, sleepy head," Jaxon said as he walked out of the kitchen with two plates in his hand. "I made us a little brunch." He handed me one of the plates that was filled with scrambled eggs, bacon, pancakes, and hash browns.

"Damn, boy, who gon' eat all of this?" I asked playfully.

"You, because you are gonna need your energy for what I got planned today." He laughed.

"Energy? Boy, this is straight up itis food. I mean, where is the fruit." He walked in the kitchen and came back with two glasses of orange juice.

"Fruit, baby." He handed me the glass, and we both laughed and started to eat.

"So what do you have planned for today?" I asked curiously.

"Something fun," he said in between bites.

"I hate to ruin your plans, but I can't go anywhere in the same outfit from yesterday," I said, pointing to the sundress I was still wearing.

"Don't worry, shorty, I got you covered." He smiled, and we continued to eat. After we finished breakfast, he led me to his bedroom and opened his closet door.

"I saw this on The Shade Room. Karrueche was spotted wearing her boyfriend's shirt, and it looked good as hell, so I figured you can turn one of my shirts into like a dress or something." I looked at him, and I could tell he was serious.

"Are you serious?" I asked in disbelief. He just smiled and started pulling out shirts.

"Go jump in the shower, and I'll have them on the bed and waiting for you. I looked at him, laughed, and went into the bathroom to shower. I couldn't believe I was in another man's house while naked. I didn't know if this was hoe behavior or not. I washed up with his Irish Spring body wash, rinsed and got out of the shower. I walked to the sink where he had an extra toothbrush waiting for me.

I looked in the mirror at myself. *I can't believe Adrian said those things to me last night.* I thought as I put the toothpaste on the bristles. I mean, I know he was drunk, but damn, a drunken word ain't nothing but a sober thought, and now I know exactly how his ass feels about me, so you know what? Fuck him. I'm going to do me.

I finished up and walked out of the bathroom with the towel wrapped around me. Going back into the bedroom, I closed the door and checked out the bunch of shirts on the bed. I looked through them and settled on a blue and white striped button-up. It hung right above my knees. I found a white belt in his closet and put it around the shirt to make it a little more fitted. I looked in the mirror, and it actually looked pretty damn good.

I opened the door to the room, and I could hear the water running in the bathroom. Jaxon was in the shower. I walked back into the living room to check on my phone. *Still no missed calls.* I guess it was for real over with Adrian and me. I just don't get it. We are supposed to be married, and he knows he was wrong for what he said to me last night. Man, fuck him then. I could feel the tears starting to well up, and I was about to let them flow when I heard the water shut off in the bathroom. I wiped my eyes and started to put my shoes on.

"Hey, let me see how it looks," he said from behind me. I stood up and turned around to show him.

"Oh. Oh my," I said in shock. Jaxon was standing there, wrapped in a towel; his body glistened from the water.

"Damn, girl. Your thick, pretty ass definitely made that work." I smiled, and I could tell I was blushing. I couldn't help but stare at his thick ass member that pushed up against the towel. I could feel myself licking my lips. "Ight, you keep looking like that, and I'm going to have you in this room begging me not to stop," he said, and I really started to blush. He laughed. "I'm going to get dressed, and then we can head out." He said and disappeared into the bedroom.

Damn, that nigga looked good. I was trying my hardest not to stare, but damn, that shit was big, and he was talking about a bitch gon' be begging. Shiiiddd, that must be some good ass dick then. *Shit, let me be cool before I wet my damn panties.* I shook those freaky ass thoughts out of my head as I heard the bedroom door open, and he walked out with a blue and white shirt and some jeans.

"Trying to match my swag, I see," I joked, and he laughed. "Yeah, bae, but something is missing."

"What?" I asked, and he tossed me a bottle of lotion.

"For your ashy knees, Mr. Brown." We both laughed hard. I put on the lotion, grabbed my things, and we headed out the door.

We rode for about an hour, but it didn't seem that long, because we spent the entire car ride cracking jokes on each other. I hadn't had this much fun with a guy in years. Adrian never understood the art of joke cracking; he was too damn emotional and would start bringing up peoples' truths to hurt them. I was having the time of my life when we pulled up to a carnival.

"You ready to have some fun?" he asked as he parked the car and started to get out.

"Hell yeah, I am," I said as I followed his lead. We walked through the gates and started our day of fun.

Adrian

I held Hazel's hips as she bounced up and down on my lap, her moans echoing off the walls as she threw her head back. "Make me cum, Adrian!" she yelled, and I started to thrust my hips up as she came down harder and faster. We fucked in an unruly manner until we both exploded in pure ecstasy. "Damn, Ajie, that shit was good," she moaned as she slid off my lap and sat next to me on the couch. "I'm hungry," she said as she laid her head on my shoulder and played with my limp penis.

"Get up in there and cook something," I said as I moved her hand and pulled up my pants.

"Ha, cook? Me?" She laughed. "How about we order some food or something?" she asked as she grabbed her phone and went to Uber Eats. Damn, I forgot that her ass couldn't cook. I remembered one time; she almost burned her apartment down while trying to boil eggs. Damn. I shook my head and stood up.

"Don't worry about it. It's some leftover dinner in here from last night." I walked into the kitchen and opened the fridge.

"Who made it? LiNa?" she asked mockingly.

"Yeah, she did. Lil' mama definitely knows how to throw down in the kitchen," I mocked back.

"Whatever," she said as she walked back to the couch.

"What's wrong with you?" I asked as I put the food on the plate.

"Nothing." She pouted. *Here we fucking go—women and their fucking games. I don't have time for this emotional shit.* I continued to make my plate as she let out a long sigh.

"Ugh, what's wrong, girl?" I asked, irritated.

"Ever since I've been here, you been throwing Lina in my face. Oh, Lina makes sure the toilet seat is up for me when she comes out the bathroom, and oh, Lina throws down in the kitchen. Well, if Lina was so fucking great, then why are you fucking me!" she yelled. I stared at her like she had lost her mind. "How do you expect me to be with you when all you do is bring up Lina?" She stared at me, waiting for an answer.

"Be with me? Girl, what the hell are you talking about?" At this point, I was completely confused.

"Aren't you and that bitch getting a divorce?" she hesitantly asked, and I laughed.

"A divorce? Are you serious?" Her silence assured me that she was being serious. "First of all, if I was getting a divorce, do you think the first thing I would do would be to jump into a new relationship? Secondly, Hazel, right now, we are just fucking and getting to know each other again. What makes you think you are someone I want to be with, or vice versa?" I asked, not trying to hurt her feelings, but trying to be real. A divorce hadn't even crossed my mind. I couldn't give up Lina, but I didn't want to end this shit with Hazel either.

"Fuck you, Adrian. This shit ain't a game. I will get my shit and move the fuck around if you're telling me this shit ain't worth my time," she said as she pushed me and started to grab her clothes.

"Let's just see where this goes. I mean, shit, if you think you can take me from my wife, then show your worth," I said as I looked down at the bulge in my pants. For some reason, all this back and forth was turning me on. I liked a girl that would fight with me, not just let me have my way. She turned back to me

"I know I can," she said as she licked her lips, walked over to me and got on her knees. I could feel my body tingle as she pulled down my pants.

Jaxon

I held on to Lina's hand as we spun around on the tilt-a-whirl. "I think I'm going to puke!" she yelled, and I definitely felt the same way. The ride finally stopped, and we wobbled off. "Again!" she screamed as she pulled me back to the line.

"No, girl. We have been on that ride five times already. I don't think my stomach is in my belly anymore." I laughed as we started to wander through the park. "We've rode every ride in here more than once. Now it's time for me to play some games," I said as I pulled her over to the basketball long shot game.

"Step right up. One in wins. Try and win a bear for the lovely lady there, just one buck." The conductor of the game gave his speech, and I gave him the dollar. He gave me three balls, and I sunk the first one into the net with no problem. "We have a winner! Pick one," he said as he pointed to the smallest bears.

"Hell naw, man. How many do I have to sink in order to get that?" I pointed to the big Tigger that hung at the top.

"All three," he said, pointing to the last two balls.

"Say less." I grabbed the first ball and followed it up with the second. They both went in, and he pulled the stuffed animal down. "For you, my lady," I said as I handed the bear to Lina. She smiled and gave me the biggest hug.

"You are awesome, Hud!"

"You bring it out of me, shorty," I said as I grabbed her and pulled her closer to me. She looked up, and I stared into her beautiful, soft, brown eyes. I could slowly see the pain draining from her eyes and being replaced with joy. I started to lean in for a kiss.

"Lina!" A voice from behind made us both spin around.

"Hey, Riley," Lina said anxiously.

"Hey, girl. Are you going to introduce me to your friend?" she quizzed, and I could hear the curiosity in her voice.

"Riley, this is Jaxon. Jaxon, this is my BFF Riley," she introduced us.

"Hey, Riley," I said with a smile.

"Oh my God," she said as she quickly pulled Lina away and left me standing with her date.

"Wassup, Jaxon? I'm Kaden," he introduced himself and we sparked up a conversation while the girls talked.

Riley Jackson

I was walking around the carnival with my boo, Kaden, when I saw my girl Lina hugged up with some nigga that was not Adrian. I walked up to her, and I could tell she was shocked. "Hey, girl. Are you going to introduce me to your friend?" I asked, and she introduced us.

"Hey, Riley," Jaxon said with a smile that almost wet my damn panties. I quickly pulled Lina out of the guys' ear range.

"Um, what the hell is going on, bitch?" I was so curious, and I knew it showed.

"Girl, listen. Some shit went down between me and Adrian, and I'm just blowing off some steam and having a little fun," she said nonchalantly like it wasn't a big deal. She glanced at Jaxon and then back at me.

"Ummhmmm, that better be the only thing you're blowing off."

"Bitch," she said with a laugh. "Shut your ass up." We laughed together and started to walk back over to the guys who were now holding more prizes. "Well, I guess this is a double date now."

"Yeah but listen. I don't want this to be the gossip of the office," she said, already knowing that I couldn't hold water.

"I got you, girl. My lips are sealed." We reached the guys, and they started talking about grabbing a bottle and heading to the shoreline that was not too far from the carnival. "Hell yeah, I'm down, but not too late because *we* gotta be at work in the morning," I said as I locked arms with Lina.

Lina (Monday Morning)

My alarm went off at six in the morning. I shut it off with the quickness and sat up on the couch. Damn, my head was pounding. What the hell was I thinking, drinking all night, knowing I had to go to fucking work? I groaned as I looked around the room. Riley was lying on the couch, and the guys were on the floor. Damn, how did we even get home? We were so fucked up.

"Damn, where am I?" Riley asked in a groggy voice.

"This is Jaxon's place," I answered as I stood up and started walking to the bathroom. "I'm gonna take a quick shower. We gotta get to work." I closed the door, undressed, and hopped into the shower. I was washing up when I heard the door open and close, the toilet seat hit the back of the toilet, and a stream of what I assumed was piss. I pulled back the curtain just for a little peek. *OMG, it's huge.* I pulled my head back quickly and held my chest. It wasn't even fully hard

"Hey, shorty, what do you want for dinner tonight?" he asked as he flushed the toilet.

"Wait, huh?" I asked, confused.

"What are you trying to eat on after work?" he repeated.

"Hud—" He cut me off.

"Aw shit, it's always bad news when you call me Hud," he said in a defeated tone.

"It's not like that. I just got a lot to really think about, and being here is distracting," I said in the best way possible. He was silent. "I think I'm going to stay at my parents' house for a few days," I said, and I could hear a sigh of relief.

"Ight, shorty. I definitely understand." He paused as he opened the door. "Oh, and by the way, Kaden and I made a run last night while you girls were sleep. I picked you up some work scrubs for today and grabbed your car from the bar." I heard the door close, and when I peeped out again, he was gone, and the scrubs were hanging on the back of the door. *Damn, he is such a great man, but he is not my husband.* I really feel like this entire situation is just infidelity to the fullest, and even though AJ hurt me, we've been together way too long for me to just jump on the first thing walking, especially over a drunken spat. I just need to get somewhere neutral, clear my head, and figure out my next move. I turned off the water, got out, and got ready for work. Riley got ready, and about thirty minutes later, we were out the door and headed to work.

Chapter Four

Hazel

I feel like a new woman, I thought as I walked into work. I spent another night with Adrian, and I swear that man was absolutely perfect—the way he looked, the way he dressed, the way he fucked, and not to mention his damn bank account. *I can't wait to take Lina's spot.* I thought to myself as I strutted to my desk. She does not deserve that man at all. I don't understand; all she had to do was eat less and wear weave. How fucking hard is that? You literally gotta be a goofy bitch to fuck that up.

"Hey, Hazel," I heard a voice from behind me. I turned around and saw Aaron standing there with a big, goofy grin on his face. *I never liked this goofy nigga.* I rolled my eyes and forced a smile.

"Yes, Aaron? What do you need?"

"I have a proposition for you," he said with a smile and then led me into his office.

"What is this about?" I asked as he closed the door.

"Adrian and Lina," he said as he sat on the edge of his desk

"What about them?" I asked, slightly irritated.

"Well, first off, I know you are screwing Adrian," he said, and it shocked me.

"And?" I asked, trying to play it cool.

"And you know he's not going to leave Lina for you," he said, and I rolled my eyes.

"What makes you say that?" I asked, amused.

"He just told me," he said, and my blood instantly started boiling.

I can't believe Adrian is trying to play me. I didn't come all this way to be looking stupid. His dad said that he was going to make sure I become a Long... Wait... Maybe he set this meeting up between me and Aaron because he doesn't like to get his own hands dirty.

"But," he continued. "I know how to change all of that." He grinned, and I could tell he had something up his sleeve. "We are going to set Lina up," he said as he rubbed his hands together.

"Did Mr. Long put you up to this?" I asked, and he nodded his head. "OK. Well, tell me the plan."

Adrian (Friday Evening)

I pulled up to the house after a long day at work. I was hoping to see Lina's car in the driveway, but it wasn't there. I parked the car and walked into our empty house. It'd been damn near a week, and Lina had not been home. As soon as I walked in the house, I became depressed. The dishes were piled high in the sink, and the garbage was running over. I walked to the fridge, and it was empty.

"Ahhhhhh!" I yelled as I slammed the fridge door and started to make my way upstairs. I opened the door and was met with the stench of dirty clothes. "Where is my wife!" I yelled as I kicked the basket over in a frustrated rage.

I didn't realize how much Lina did when she was here. She always got home from work before me and made sure the house was together. I missed seeing her smiling face while she stood in the kitchen, preparing dinner. I missed smelling her scent in the middle of the night when she's sleeping. *I fucking miss my wife.* I grabbed my phone and looked at the last message she sent me.

Lina: I'm ok. I just need to clear my head.

I read it over and over. *Damn, I must have really hurt her. Since that night, she hasn't answered my phone calls or texts.* I put my head in my hands, and I could feel the tears filling my eyes. "God," I started to pray out loud. "Please bring my wife back to me. I know I messed up, but I see now that I can't live without her—" I was cut off by the doorbell. "Who the fuck?" I said as I stood up, wiped my face, and dragged myself down the stairs.

I hope it ain't Hazel. Her clingy, freak-body ass is getting on my last damn nerve, I thought as I looked at the camera to see who was at the door. To my surprise, it was my dad. *Oh, great. Here we go with this shit,* I thought as I pulled the door open.

"Hey, son," he said as he pushed his way into the house. "I see your little maid hasn't come home yet," he said as he shoved a beer into my hand. I opened it and took a drink.

"Dad, please. I don't want to hear that shit today," I said, not caring about being disrespectful because this was my house.

"Hey, don't take your frustrations out on me," he said as he started to drink his beer. "Have you heard from her?" he asked, and I laughed, not believing that he was really that concerned.

"Not since Monday night when she texted me," I said as I sat on the couch and continued to drink my sorrows away.

"Son let me be the first to tell you that you married a weak woman. I don't know what you said to her, but it should not have been enough to make her stay away this long. If that girl really loved you, she would be back in this house, washing your smelly drawls with a smile on her face." He paused, waiting for me to say something, but I just continued to drink my beer.

"Just look at your mother. I've put her through hell. I've said mean things to her. Hell, I've even been caught cheating a few times, but she stays because she loves me." I laughed.

"No, she stays because she loves the lifestyle, Dad."

He stared at me. "Exactly, son. Your mother is Long material; she doesn't let the simple things of life ruin her comfort.

Your wife is not Long material at all." I sat tensely as I listened to my father talk about how he cheated and how my mother dealt with it. I remembered seeing him with my nannies and his secretaries. I had always vowed to myself that when I got married, I would be a different husband.

I had literally become my dad, talking down on my wife, making her feel like she was my servant instead of my wife, cursing her and starting fights for no reason, and then the ultimate betrayal. I'd been cheating on her since she left. What the fuck was wrong with me? "Dad, I'm really over this conversation." He finished his beer and grabbed another one.

"You know who is Long material though? That damn Hazel. Her dad reached out to me, and he said that he would not mind having you as a son-in-law." He paused and looked me square in the eye. "Her family has a lot of money, son, and if we join together with them, we can really move our firm to the next level," he said, and I could tell he was beyond serious.

"Well, why don't you marry her then, Dad?" I scoffed, clearly irritated at this whole situation.

"Listen, son. I'm just trying to help you. How long are you going to let this girl bring you down, huh!" he started to yell. "She doesn't bring shit to our family table! Just take and take! I've been dealing with this bitch for three years, and you went against my wishes and married her and now look!" He stood up. "You out here fucking Hazel any damn way, so I don't fucking get what the big deal is. Just know that you are this fucking close to getting cut the fuck off like your damn brother." He walked to the door and opened it. "You need to handle this shit, or I will handle it for you!" he said as he walked out. I went to the door and slammed it behind him.

"Fuuuuccckkkkkkk!" I yelled, angry and helpless. I ran upstairs and grabbed my phone. I called Lina. She was the only person that could talk me down after I had it out with my dad, but I didn't get an answer, so I called her mother.

Lina

I sat at my desk, scrolling through my Facebook and looking at old pictures of Adrian and me back when we were happy. I came across one of our beautiful wedding pictures; we were standing at the altar, exchanging our vows. Where did we go wrong, man? I mean, he stood before me, our families, and God and confessed that he would care for me, be there for me. He promised that in times when I was down, he would cry for me, and if shit ever got real, he would die for me. He promised to give me love and happiness through the good and the bad. I mean, damn, he was supposed to live for me. Where the hell did things go so wrong? I needed this Adrian back.

"Hey, Lina. You have a package at the front desk." Sam beamed as she walked into the office with a smile.

"For real?" I asked as I walked to the receptionist's desk with Sam right on my heels. When I got there, I saw this big vase full of pink Asiatic lilies, pink and red roses, purple wax flowers, and Alstroemeria.

"Damn, I guess Adrian is finally trying to make up." Sam hummed as she smelled the flowers. "These are fucking beautiful," she continued as I grabbed the card.

I opened it up, and it read in bold letters: **To the most beautiful girl I ever met. I didn't know what your favorite flower was, so I sent them all xoxo JH**

I smiled and looked at Sam. "Girl, AJ is not that damn romantic." I grabbed my flowers and started to walk to the time clock.

"Shit, could have fooled me. Let me see the card," she said as she tried to take the card from my hand. I pulled back right as Riley and Ollie walked up.

"Beautiful flowers. Did Adrian finally come to his fucking senses?" Ollie asked as he snatched the card out of my hand. "Who the hell is JH?" he asked in his flamboyant voice.

"Girl, did Jaxon send those?" Riley blurted, and I looked at her sharply, but it was too late.

"Jaxon, as in the nigga that was at the bar last week?" Ollie asked, looking at me like I had lost my mind.

"It's not even that deep." I sighed, not trying to deal with the big *you and Adrian are supposed to be together forever* speech.

"Not that deep, bitch? This bouquet was almost a hundred dollars. You must have fucked him real good," he said as he started swerving his hips.

"Lina, no!" Sam exclaimed, disappointed.

"First of all, I didn't fuck him, so please don't put those bad vibes into the air," I said, getting slightly irritated as both Sam and Ollie stared at me with judging eyes. "See, that's why I didn't want y'all asses to know. I don't need you judging me!" I said as I stormed out of the building and walked to my car.

I pulled up to my parents' house about fifteen minutes later and walked into the living room. "Hey, Mom, are you here?" I asked as I set the flowers on the living room table and walked into the kitchen.

"Hey, baby," she said as she stood over the stove, cooking dinner.

"Whatever you are making, it sure does smell good," I said as I kissed her on the cheek.

"Your dad wanted soul food tonight, so I'm making some oxtails, baked macaroni, and greens," she said as she stirred the pot of greens. My mother was beautiful; she was pretty much me, just a little older, a little wiser, and a little thicker than me. "That husband of yours called again, and he sounds so miserable. I could have sworn he was crying," she said as she walked to the sink to wash her hands.

"Well, Mom, that's on him. I'm done," I said unsurely.

"Darlina Bailey, how can you say that? It's only been a year. Once married, you two are bonded under God. There is no such thing as being done. Married people go through things, but you vowed under God that it was going to be through the good and the bad. You have to fight for your marriage, girl." She'd started with her lecture, and I was already over it. My mother was very religious, and she didn't believe in divorce, so I knew talking to her was going to be like talking to a brick wall.

"I understand what you are saying, Ma, but I've been dealing with so much from Adrian this last year, and I just needed a little break," I said, trying to ease out of the conversation.

"Girl, a break is thirty minutes to an hour. You have been here for a week now, and don't think I haven't seen you sneaking out with that boy. What's his name?" She paused. "Oh yeah,

Hudson. His daddy was a whore—excuse my language, Lord," she said as he put her hand in the air. "Adrian is your husband, girl. You need to be home, trying to make it work with him." She went back to the stove to check on the greens.

"I hear you, Ma, but you have to understand, I am unhappy there. Everyday being in his presence is miserable. I can't wear my hair the way I want. I can't dress the way I want. He doesn't even like my friends. It's like when I'm with him, I have to be everybody but myself," I said, trying to plead my case.

"Yeah, baby, well maybe you should have really got to know him before you married him," she said, and it felt like a stab in the gut. I knew she didn't mean it in a rude way, but sometimes, the truth has to be spoken, and sometimes, the truth hurts.

"You're right, Mom," I said as I walked out of the kitchen and up to my old room. I pulled out my phone and dialed Adrian's number.

Adrian

I sat on the couch with a bottle in one hand and Hazel's head in the other. Her wet, warm mouth felt so good on my hard dick. I groaned and took another swig from the bottle. *Maybe I should just marry this bitch.* My drunken thoughts were interrupted by my cell phone ringing. I looked over, and it was Lina's picture on the screen.

"Hold on. Hold on," I said as I pushed Hazel off and grabbed my phone. "Hey, baby," I answered as I walked into the guest room and closed the door.

"Hey, wassup? My momma said you called." Her voice was low and dull.

"Yeah, baby, I miss you so much. When are you coming home?" I asked, hopeful that she was going to say tonight.

"I don't know right now, Adrian. That shit you said that night really got me thinking, and maybe..." She paused.

"Baby, I didn't mean any of that," I said before she could continue. "I was stupid, and this week has shown me that I cannot live without you. Please come home to me, baby," I pleaded, and she grew silent. "Lina," I said so low that I barely heard myself. I could hear her sobbing.

"I love you, Adrian, but I can't help but think that you don't love me. You married me out of spite because of your father, and you shoot me down every chance you get," she said.

"I can change. I need you. Please, let's just talk it out. Come home, and I'll get us dinner, or we can go out to that restaurant you really like," I begged.

"I'm busy tonight, but we can meet up tomorrow," she said, and I could feel my heart leap.

"OK, tomorrow it is." The phone was quiet.

"I love you," she said and hung up.

"Yesss!" I yelled as I walked back out into the living room, completely forgetting that Hazel was there, still drinking on the couch. I threw her a blanket and a pillow and then went upstairs to my room. She followed me.

"What the hell is going on?" she asked in an angered voice.

"I'm meeting with Lina tomorrow to try and work things out," I said, knowing that it was not the right thing to say.

"Are you serious?" she asked, surprised.

"Why are you so surprised, Hazel? She is my wife."

She looked at me and walked back into the living room. I closed and locked my door behind her. *Bitch ain't about to kill me in my sleep.*

Hazel

I stood with my ear to the door, listening to Adrian's conversation with Lina; he was in there, pleading and crying like a little bitch. I heard him say *tomorrow it is,* and I walked back to the couch. "Oh, so he's meeting her ass tomorrow. This nigga," I said as I poured myself another drink. He walked out shortly after and threw a blanket and pillow on the couch and walked upstairs to his room. I followed him, and we had a small confrontation. I was so upset that all I could do was storm back into the living room.

"Who the hell does he think he is? I've been here every fucking day this week, letting him fuck me until I was raw, and now he is talking about going back to her," I said angrily to myself. *I got something for both their asses.* I picked up my phone and texted Aaron.

Me: How is the plan coming along?

Aaron: It's being worked out, don't worry about it.

I put my phone down and laid on the couch. *I hope Aaron's plan is cool, but if not, I got a little something up my sleeve. I need Lina completely out of the way.* I heard the bedroom door open, and Adrian walked down the stairs, naked.

"You're gonna come hop on this motherfucker one last time?" he asked with that smile that I couldn't resist. I didn't say anything. I just got up and followed him upstairs.

Jaxon

I pulled up to Lina's parents' house, and she silently closed the door and ran to the car. She got in and smiled. "Thanks for the flowers," she said as she kissed me on the cheek.

"Anything for you, queen," I said as I put the car in drive. "Where you wanna go?"

"I just wanna go back in time and rethink my life," she said.

"What's going on, shorty?" I asked, but I then felt stupid because I know her situation.

"I talked to Adrian today, and it was just weird, hearing him with real compassion and concern in his voice…" She paused. "I'm sorry, Hud. I know you don't wanna hear about this," she said, and we both sat quietly. I knew this day would come. I really liked this woman, but at the end of the day, I knew the situation.

"Shorty, look. I knew what I was getting into with you. I'm just happy to have had the little bit of time I did with you. I was never here to steal you from your husband; I was just here to remind you that you are an amazingly, beautiful, strong, loving, and intelligent woman, and you deserve to be loved and respected. I don't think we ran into each other twice by accident. You were at a point in your life where you needed to be reminded that you only have one life to live, and you will survive, living it your way and not your husband's way. I'm just happy I was able to have these moments with you." I poured my heart out to her while she sat, looking out the window. I could see the tears running down her face through the reflection. "Just because you are going back to your husband doesn't mean we can't still be friends, so, girl, stop all that crying," I said, trying to reassure her that everything would work out.

"That's just it. I don't know if I want to go back. I'm crying because I'm so torn right now. I am genuinely happy when I am with you. I mean, some nights, my jaws hurt from smiling so hard. I don't know if I want to go back into that negative atmosphere. I feel like weights have been lifted off my shoulder, and I am finally free. But that's my husband, and I made a vow to love him for better and for worse, through the good and the bad. I just don't know what to do." She stopped talking, and we sat in silence. I didn't know what to say. It was just a hard situation, and as much as I would like to, I didn't have the answers.

"Well, shorty, let's just enjoy this last night together, drink something, smoke something, vibe out to the music, and let the night take us wherever it takes us," I said as I pulled out a pre-rolled blunt and lit it. She grabbed it from me and took a few long puffs.

"Yeah, I just wish God would give me a sign." I watched her as she zoned out and started dancing to the music. I would be lying to myself if I said that I was ready to let her go. She was the only woman that I could see myself with for real, but she wasn't mine. She passed the blunt back to me, and we continued into our night.

Lina

It was the middle of the night when I was pulled from my sleep. I looked over at Jaxon, and he was sleeping on the other couch. *You can't keep doing this Lina; you are a married woman, and this is too close to cheating.* I heard the voice in my head, but it didn't sound like me. Standing up, I walked into the bathroom and stared at myself in the mirror. *Lina, you have to go home. This isn't right, and this isn't you. You love Adrian,* the voice said again. I could feel an ache creep across my forehead. I quickly turned on the water and splashed my face. *Go home, Lina.* I held my head as the voice grew louder. It felt as if my brain was going to explode. *Go home, Lina! Go home, go home, go home!*

I woke up in a cold sweat, gasping for air. I was still laying on the couch. It was at that point I realized I must have been dreaming. I looked around, and Jaxon was sleeping on the other couch. Grabbing my phone, I quickly ordered an Uber. I put on my shoes and grabbed my things. My Uber was a few minutes away. I grabbed a pen and paper and wrote a note to Jaxon, and then I left. Sliding into the backseat, I headed to my parents' house to get my car. But then I thought about the dream. *Go home Lina.* The words crossed my mind.

"Excuse me. Can I change my destination?" I asked as I pulled out my phone to put in my address. "I have to go home," I said weakly.

The drive was quiet, which left me to nothing but my thoughts. *What should I say when I get there? Are we gonna be able to work through this? Do I really love him? Hell, does he really love me? What about Jaxon? Did I lead him on?* My mind filled with questions as I stared out the window. Visions of Jaxon flashed through my mind. He was such a great guy, and he deserves to have a single woman with no drama. Leaving him is best. I have feelings for him, but I love Adrian. *But is it crazy that I think I might love Jaxon as well?* This last week has been amazing. We've been out on dates, we've cooked together, we've spent nights up just talking and really getting to know each other, and we talked about things that I wouldn't have even dreamed of talking about with Adrian. I feel like I bared my soul to him this last week, and he accepted every part.

"Hey, are you OK back there?" the driver asked, bringing me out of my thoughts.

"I'm just thinking about something that my best friend is going through." I replied and she looked at me through the rearview mirror.

"What's going on?" she inquired.

"Well, she's been with this one guy for like three years, and she loves him to death. But since they've been together, she has lost herself. Dressing the way he wants her to dress, wearing her hair the way he wants, and when she tries to just be herself, he lashes out on her. But then says he loves her. Now recently, they got into this huge fight where he drunkenly said some beyond hurtful things, so she left and has been hanging with a new guy. He's the complete opposite. He loves the way she dresses, the way she wears her hair, and when she's with him, she feels like no one else matters, but…" I paused.

"But she feels like since she's been with the other guy for so long that she is obligated to go back to him," she completed my sentence.

"Yeah, exactly. She loves him, but now she thinks she might be falling in love with the new guy," I continued.

"Damn, that is a lot," she said. "Well, girl, all I gotta say is this. You only have one life to live. You are either gonna live it miserably or happily; the choice is yours. To be honest, love is like cake. You love chocolate cake so much that you never wanted to try anything else, but shit, how will you know if you like cheesecake if you don't at least try it?"

I sat in the back seat, perplexed.

"That actually makes pretty good sense. Thank you," I said, grateful.

"No problem, girl. Us women have to stick together." She paused. "Tell your friend that at the end of the day, you gotta be nice for what to these niggas?" she said as she pulled into my driveway. *Damn, nice for what to these niggas? That would be a catchy ass song.*

"You enjoy the rest of your night, and be safe out here," I said as I got out of the car and walked up to the door. I felt around anxiously for my keys before remembering they were at my parents' house. "Damn it." I muttered while ringing the doorbell. I heard some moving inside, and after like five minutes, the door swung open. We stood, looking at each other for a moment, and then he pulled me in for a hug.

"I've missed you, girl." He pulled me inside.

Adrian

I was woken out of my sleep by someone ringing the doorbell. I looked out of my bedroom window and saw Lina standing at the door. I quickly jumped up and woke Hazel.

"Hey, wake up. You gotta go!" I said as I yanked her out the bed.

"Why? What the hell is going on?" she asked confusedly.

"My wife is home," I said as I pulled her down the stairs, gathering her things piece by piece.

"Adrian, it's one in the morning," she whined.

"I'm sorry. I'll call you," I said as I shoved her out the back door and then walked to the front and opened the door for Lina. She stood there, looking beautiful, and I didn't know what to say. I could see Hazel out the corner of my eye, trying to sneak to her car, so I pulled Lina in for a close hug.

"I've missed you, girl," I said sincerely.

Once Hazel made it to her car, I pulled Lina inside. "Damn, girl, you are a sight for sore eyes," I said as I tried to kiss her, but she moved back. "I guess I deserve that, bae. I am so sorry, and I promise to do everything I can to make it up to you." I paused. "I need you, Lina. You are my wife, and I love you." She looked at me, and I couldn't tell what she was thinking. I leaned in to kiss her, and she didn't pull away. I kissed her longingly, but her mood was stiff and cold.

I pulled back and she looked away. "I know I have a lot of work to do, and I promise I will do everything in my power to fix this." I didn't know what else to say. It suddenly felt like this was a stranger in my house. She looked up at me and stared into my eyes. It seemed as if she was trying to read my soul. She reached up and softly caressed my face before pulling me into a kiss.

The sweet smell of her, sent an exciting chill through my body. I kissed her cheek and moved down to her neck. My manhood quivered for her. I needed her bad. Laying her on the couch, I slowly pulled down her pants and admired her matured bush. I was prepared for her to push me off, but she didn't, which was a good sign. Gently pushing her legs open, I leaned in and started to nibble on her thigh. She let out a small moan, which turned me on. I spread her legs wider and stuck my tongue inside of her slit, flicking my tongue and softly nibbling on her pearl. I wanted to make her feel good. I wanted to make her feel so good that she'd never leave me again. She moaned as I sucked, licked and did everything possible to make her cum. She grabbed my head and exploded into my mouth.

"Oh my God!" she exclaimed, and it turned me on. I pulled out my stiff joint and slid it inside her wet walls. Her thickness was such a comfort, especially since I'd been fucking Hazel.

"Damn, Lina," I groaned as I stroked. "I've missed you," I said as I hungrily sucked on her breast. She moaned again, and I stroked faster. I tried to hold on for as long as I could, but her wet, warm spot sucked me in, and before I knew it, I was filling her up with my juices. I pulled out and rolled onto the floor.

"Damn, girl, I'm so happy you're home."

Lina

I laid on the couch as Adrian thrust in and out of me. It was at this moment that I knew how hurt I. I couldn't even enjoy it. It felt awkward, laying under him, pretending to moan. He was enjoying every stroke, but my mind wasn't in it. At this point, I was completely over this cake, but I couldn't leave this relationship without at least trying to make it work. Adrian emptied himself inside of me and then rolled to the floor. Moments later, I could hear him snoring. I rolled my eyes and got up off the couch. Walking into the bathroom, I grabbed a towel to clean myself out. I walked out of the bathroom and headed upstairs into the bedroom.

I took off my clothes, put on a nightgown and laid in the bed. As I got comfortable, I started to think about Jaxon—his smooth, chocolate skin, his sexy ass lips, and that smile that had been having me wet for an entire week. Thinking about him turned me on. I opened my legs to feel how wet I was, and I was dripping. I started to rub myself with the thoughts of him standing in that towel; visions of the towel falling invaded my head. I closed my eyes and watched him stroke himself as he walked over to me, licking his lips and flicking his tongue at me. The thought made my pearl swell, and before I knew it, my back was arching, and I was cumming all over my hand.

"Fuck," I said to myself as I tried to catch my breath. I heard the stairs creak, and I quickly closed my legs, right as Adrian walked into the room.

"So you're just gonna leave me on the floor like that?" He laughed and climbed into the bed with me. He kissed me on the forehead, got under the covers, and went to sleep. I moved closer to the edge and turned my back to him. My mind wandered aimlessly before I drifted off to sleep.

Riley

My eyes rolled in the back of my head as I bounced up and down on Kaden's long, hard anaconda. I leaned over and started to kiss his full lips. He moaned inside of my mouth and rubbed his hands up and down the spine of my back.

"Yeah, girl, you better ride this donkey dick," he moaned, and I stopped in mid stroke and started to laugh.

"Please, do not say that ever again." He opened his eyes and stared up at me and started to laugh as well. He then flipped me over onto my back and got on top.

"Girl, you better take this big donkey dick," he joked as he long stroked me.

"Awww shit!" I screamed. "Yes, fuck me with that donkey dick, daddy," I moaned out loud as I felt myself explode all over him. He held my hips and continued to stroke.

"Yeah, baby, cum all over me. I love feeling your juices run down my body," he moaned and continued to slam harder inside of me. I couldn't control my body, and I began to cum again.

"Awww my God!" I yelled as I grabbed his shoulders and dug my nails into his skin.

"Aww shit!" he yelled as he pulled out of me and came all over my stomach. He continued to stroke himself until his entire nut was out. He got up and grabbed a wet towel off of the dresser and tossed it at me, and I wiped myself clean and gave it back to him.

"Damn, nigga, that was some good ass dick," I said while pulling my panties up. He smiled and started to move his hips side to side, making his limp member swing wildly.

"Yeah, this that *make you cum five times* type of dick," he joked as he lay back in the bed and pulled me closer to him. "Why you putting those barriers back on? I need that pussy free for round three." He laughed as he smacked me on the ass. *Round three? This nigga is crazy as hell; we've been fucking all damn night, and I am completely exhausted.* I stared at his naked, russet, reddish-brown body as it glistened with sweat. *Damn, he is fine as hell.*

"I really enjoyed hanging with your friend..." He paused. "But isn't she the one that's married to the lawyer guy?" he hesitantly asked.

"Yeah," I replied. "But her husband is a complete asshole, and he doesn't appreciate her worth. And I honestly think he's cheating on her with this no body having, flat-booty, if-I-was-a-boy head ass chick," I joked

"So, are you justifying cheating? Because if that's how you feel problems should be handled in a marriage, then maybe we should end this now." He chided, and I sat up and looked at him.

"Wait. What's happening right now?" I asked, confused.

"You are sitting here, telling me that it is OK for your friend to be with another nigga because her husband is an asshole," he snapped, and I just looked at him. I could see the anger in his eyes, and I could tell that this conversation was bringing up something deeper.

"Listen," I started. "Lina is one of my good friends, and yes, she is married. But her husband has been treating her like an ugly stepchild. I haven't seen her smile this much since I've met her. And yes, the circumstances are bad, but everyone deserves a little happiness. You might not agree, but who are we to judge?" I finished and rubbed his cheek. "What's going on though, bae?" I asked, hoping he would open up. He sat silently and then got up and walked into the bathroom and closed the door. I shook my head, stood up, and started to get dressed.

I really liked this guy, but every time I tried to really get to know him, he shuts down. I can see it in his eyes that he has been through some shit, and that's what attracts me to him the most. He is broken, and I know I can fix him. I heard the door open, and I looked up.

"Where are you going?" he asked in a confused tone.

"When you walked off, I figured we were done," I glumly spoke as I stood up.

"I just went to piss, girl." He laughed and pulled me into a hug. "I like you, and I'm not trying to argue over a situation that has nothing to do with us," he said as he sat down on the bed and pulled me into his lap.

"Kaden, I really like you, and I want us to work…" I paused, trying to word my thoughts right. "But we are not going to work if you keep leaving me out in the dark and running away instead of opening up. I want to love you, but how can I do that if I don't know you?" I asked as I pointed my finger against his chest right above his heart. He looked me in my eyes and pulled me into a kiss. Our tongues swirled in passion, and I could feel his hands traveling up and down my body. His member started to harden as he gripped my ass. I pulled back.

"What's wrong?" He breathed lustfully.

"You are trying to distract the conversation, and I'm not having that. If you really want to have a relationship with me, I need you to be real with me." I stood up and threw his underwear at him. "Now cover up and get real with me."

He stared at me. I folded my arms and stared back at him. He smiled at me and started to put on his drawls.

"Come here, baby." He held out his hands, and I walked over to him. He grabbed me, pulled me next to him on the bed, and stared into my eyes. "I haven't always been this guy. There was a point in my life where I was full of so much rage, so much hatred, that all I could do was close myself up and…" He stopped and looked away. I caressed his face and turned him back toward my gaze.

"I am here. Open up to me," I said with a reassuring smile. He sighed.

"Like I said, I haven't always been this guy; there was a point in my life where I was a completely different man…."

I woke up the next morning, and all I could think about was Kaden's story. He was not lying when he said he was a different man, but even though the dark parts of his past kind of scared me. Hearing about it just made me want to love him even more. I stared at him as he slept. He seemed at peace now that he had gotten those words off his chest. I heard my phone notification go off. I got up and walked over to my phone. It was from Lina.

Lina: Riley I did something stupid

Me: Aw shit, did you and Jaxon finally knock boots (wet drip emoji)

Lina: No I went back home to Adrian (face palm emoji)

Me: WHAT! Girl why???? (Shocked emoji)

Lina: Because he's my husband and I guess I gotta give him another chance (rolling eyes emoji)

Me: Rotfl (laughing-crying emoji) ok sis

Lina: But now I'm in this house and I am losing my damn mind, please come grab me, so I can run quickly out of this house and pick my car up from my parents.

Me: Ight let me get dressed; I'm at Kaden's crib so I'll be a few

I got out of the bed and went into the bathroom and hopped in the shower. I couldn't help but think back to last night. After Kaden told me his past, we made sweet, passionate love, and he didn't pull out. I mean, I was on birth control, but the fact that he felt that comfortable told me that he might really be the one. I turned off the shower, got out, walked to the sink, and brushed my teeth.

He doesn't even know that I'm on birth control, so was that his way of telling me he wants a baby, I thought as I finished up, walked back into the room, and started to get dressed. I grabbed my phone to finish texting Lina.

    Lina: Awe ok. I like Kaden, you guys are cute together (Smile emoji)

    Me: Yeah, sis I think I might love him (Heart emoji)

    Lina: Just don't jump into marriage unless you know he's not an Adrian (crying emoji)

    Me: Bitch I'm dead (Skull emoji) I'm leaving out girl, see you in about twenty.

    I kissed Kaden on the forehead, grabbed my things, and headed out. I sent him a text to his phone, assuring him that I was not running away. I jumped in my car and headed toward Lina's place.

    I can't believe she went back home to Adrian. He doesn't deserve her or her beautiful soul. I'm so happy to be friends with Lina, and I honestly think Jaxon is the best man for her. But until Lina recognizes her own worth, she will always return to Adrian's whack ass.

Chapter Five

Adrian (Saturday Morning)

I woke up and rolled over, hoping I was going to be able to slide into my baby, but the bed was empty. I sat up and rubbed my eyes. I could smell bacon in the air, and I heard music playing downstairs. *Damn, this is what the hell I am talking about. I'm so happy to have my girl home that I don't know what to do.* I rolled out of bed and headed downstairs. Lina was sitting on the couch, eating.

"Damn, bae. Breakfast smells good," I said as I walked into the kitchen and opened the microwave, looking for my plate. *Damn, where my food at?* I looked on the stove and saw a corner of eggs still in the skillet and one slice of bacon on a napkin. *Well, I guess I gotta make my own shit up,* I angrily thought to myself as I grabbed a plate and scooped the food on there. "Hey, bae, is this all you made!" I yelled from the kitchen, but she didn't reply.

I grabbed a fork and walked into the living room and sat next to her on the couch. She instantly got up with her empty plate and headed into the kitchen while looking down at her phone. *Damn, is it me, or is her vibe icy as hell?* I thought to myself as she walked back into the living room and sat on the other couch, still looking at her phone. I started to eat the little bit of food on my plate when, out of nowhere, she started laughing loud as hell. I looked at her, but she didn't look up.

"Hey, babe, what's funny?" I asked, wanting to laugh with

her.

"Oh nothing, just something Riley sent me."

"When did you and Riley become buddy-buddy? I inquired after remembering how she used to talk about how irritating she was.

"Yeah, things change," she nonchalantly replied, and I could tell she wasn't paying me any real attention, because her reply didn't make any sense.

"What's wrong with you?" I asked, slightly irritated. She finally looked up at me.

"There is nothing wrong with me, hun. Is there something wrong with you?" She stared at me, and it was like she was staring into my soul. I looked into her eyes, and I could tell she was different. I guessed I took too long to answer because she stood up with her phone and walked right past me. I watched as she went up the stairs. I could hear her moving around, and then the sound of the bathroom door close. Shortly after, I could hear the water running in the shower.

After I finished eating, I walked into the kitchen, did the dishes, and cleaned off the counters. *This shit is different.* I walked back into the living room and started to straighten up. I heard the bedroom door open, and Lina walked down the stairs, looking good as hell. She was just wearing jeans and a top, but she had a glow about her. She had her braids pulled up into two knots on her head. Her earrings shingled as she walked past me. She grabbed her charger and headed toward the door.

"Where are you going?" I asked, standing up and walking over to her.

"I have to go pick up my car," she said dryly as she glared at her phone.

"Damn, girl, you not even going to look at me?" I asked as I placed my hand over the phone.

Finally, she looked up. "Huh? Oh…" She paused, and I could tell she was trying to remember what I asked. "I am going to pick up my car from my parents' house," she said with a forced smile.

"Oh, OK, cool. I'll drive you," I said as I walked to the couch to put on my shoes.

"No, I got a ride. Thank you though," she said as she opened the front door.

"Bae, hol—" She cut me off.

"Baby, maybe you should stop at the gym today; you are getting a little round."

I sat in shock as she walked out of the door.

I can't believe this little bitch. Did she really just try to come at me like that? I walked into the guest room and looked in one of the mirrors. Damn, I guess eating all that fast food in the past week with Hazel is catching up with me. But damn, she didn't have to call me out like that. She fucking hurt my feelings man. *This shit is real fucking different.*

Riley

I sat in the car, waiting for Lina. She walked out the house, smiling, and jumped in the passenger seat. "Hey, girl!" she exclaimed and kissed me on the cheek.

"Don't *hey, girl* me. What the hell are you doing back here?" I asked as I pulled off and headed toward her mom's place.

"Girl..." She paused. "Why the hell am I here? Like, this shit is so dead. I'm just not even feeling being in the same room with him." She sighed. "He is so damn irritating and clingy; it's making my skin crawl. Like, damn, get off me and let me breathe." I laughed at her as she wiped her arms as if something was crawling on her. "I mean, he's damn near smothering me." She laughed.

"Damn, girl, you've only been home for one night," I said, trying to reason with her.

"One night too damn long, and girl, his ass is getting fat. Like, damn, really nigga? I leave for a week, and you just let yourself go," she said as she pulled down the visor to apply lipstick. "The house was a damn mess, kitchen was full of dishes, clothes were piled up in the baskets, and the garbage hadn't even been taken out. I hope he realizes how much I kept that house in order," she said as she pulled out her phone and started to take selfies. We got to a light, and she got close to me, and we took a picture together.

I liked hanging with her. I used to feel like the odd man out because she, Sam, and Ollie were so close, but they hadn't really

117

talked since the little incident with the flowers. "Hey, have you talked to Sam or Ollie?" I asked.

"Nope. I've been just trying to keep to myself, sorting out my own shit without others' opinions," she said as she scrolled through her phone.

"Yeah, I feel you. I really didn't like the way they were judging you at the time clock. I mean, damn, that nigga has been overdoing his part for a while now." My text notification went off, and I paused to answer the message from Kaden. "I mean, from him standing you up at the club, picking a fight with you, and then that new chick at his job been taking little jabs at you. I know they must be fuc—"

"Hold up, hold up, hold up. Bitch, pause. I am going to need you to run that shit back," she said as she twirled her finger in the air in a rewinding motion. "What new chick?"

"Wait. You didn't know?" I asked as I grabbed my phone and looked for the page. "Nate added her, and you know I'm the crazy ex that still stalks his ass, so shit, I added her too," I said as I handed her the phone. "That's her with Adrian's dad, smiling all hard and shit like she just won the lottery.

"And then she's posting shit like, *if my man tells me he wants me in the gym, I'm going.* So clearly, he's running his mouth to somebody about y'all issues."

She sat quietly for a moment, just scrolling through the girl's page.

"Hazel," she finally said. "She looks kind of familiar," She shrugged. "But I don't care. He can do whatever he wants; my life will go on. And for this little hoe and her status, she can talk down all she wants. She ain't trying to really catch these hands though," she said with a laugh and handed me the phone back.

"Yeah, because if she was really about that life, she would have added you."

"Exactly, lil' biiittccchh," she said, and we both laughed and started talking shit.

"Hey, have you talked to Jaxon yet?"

"Naw, not yet. I left him a note when I left last night, and he ain't called me…" She paused, and I could tell she was feeling some type of way. "He understands the situation, but I miss him." She said as we pulled up to her mother's house. "Thanks, girl," she added as she got out the car. "Hey, let's do lunch," she suggested as she closed the door and leaned up against the window.

"You just don't want to go back home with Adrian," I joked.

"Is it that obvious?" She asked with a smirk.

I laughed. "Yea, I'm down. Wherever is fine. I'll follow you there," I replied, and she smiled, shook her head, and jogged to her car. She started it up, pulled out the driveway, and I followed her down the street.

Jaxon

I sat on my couch, looking at the note Lina left. I couldn't believe she was gone, just like that. I balled the note up and threw it across the room. "Damn, man!" I yelled to myself. I know I told her that I was happy with this little bit of time, but really, I would rather have all of her time. I mean, I'm really not trying to take her from her husband, but she deserves so much more than what he has been giving her. I can love her a lot better than what he's doing. But I guess it's too late, and my chance has passed.

Samantha

I walked into the grocery store to get some fresh fruit and vegetables for my smoothie, and as I neared the produce, I saw a familiar face. "Hey, Adrian," I said, and he turned around.

"Hey, Sam, how are you?" he asked.

"I'm doing great. How are you?" I replied.

"I'm doing OK," he said with a forced smile.

"Where is Lina? Is she here with you?" I asked as I looked around. "No, she's out with Riley, and I guess she will be home later," he said as he shrugged his shoulders. "That's if she's coming home," he said in a defeated tone.

I sat there, wishing I had the right words to say. "You know what, Adrian? I really don't know what's going on between you and Lina, but you two are strong, and I know you guys will work through it." He smiled.

"Thank you, Sam. I needed to hear those words. She's finally back home, and believe me when I tell you, that was the longest week ever. Being without her was hard, but since she's been back, we just have not been connecting," he said and shook his head. "I really don't know what to do. I mean, I get it. I fucked up, but the cold shoulder that I am getting from her is unbearable. I just want the love back in my house." I could see the sorrow in his eyes.

121

"You know what? I am going to talk to her. You guys are great together, and I want to make sure you two stay together," I assured him.

"Thank you, Sam. I really appreciate it," he said, and we parted ways.

I thought about what Adrian said. I didn't know that Lina wasn't living at home. Why she wouldn't tell me that was beyond me. And damn, what the hell did Adrian do that had her not coming home for an entire week? I mean, the last thing I remembered was him standing her up at the bar. What the hell happened after that, and why the hell had she not talked to me about it? Damn, I was her best friend, but now she was hanging with Riley and shit? What the hell?

I finished shopping and loaded the groceries into the trunk. I got in the car and called Lina, and she picked up on the third ring. "Hello."

"Hey, girl, what's going on?" I asked, hoping she would talk to me.

"Nothing, girl, just out and about, running errands. What's going on?" she asked dryly.

"Nothing. I realized we hadn't really talked much since the incident at the club, and I wanted to know how you were doing." I could hear her sigh on the other side.

"Girl, it's been a lot going on."

"Well, why haven't you talked to me about it?" I asked, a little upset.

"Because I really didn't feel like being judged or told to suck it up because it's Adrian," she said, and I immediately felt offended.

"Why do you think I would judge you?" I asked in a defensive tone.

"Because that's what you do. I mean, I love you to death, but sometimes…" She stopped.

"No. Sometimes, what, Lina?" I asked, upset.

"See, look at you, getting upset for no reason. This is why I didn't tell you." I sat silently, and then I realized she was right.

"I'm sorry, sis. You are right. I do overdo it sometimes. I promise I won't overreact. Just let me in on what's been going on," I said. She sighed and started to tell me everything leading up to this point.

"OK, now you are all up to date," she said, and I sat in a state of shock.

"I can't believe you've been shacking up with another man, and you are married. How can you do that to Adrian?" I blurted out without thinking.

"See what I mean? This nigga has been dogging me out, treating me every which way, and you taking his side. You are supposed to be my friend. Even if I am in the wrong, you are supposed to be on my side—"

"Lina," I tried to cut her off.

"No, don't Lina me. You act like I said I was fucking Jaxon or something. All we did was talk, and for a week, I felt like how a woman is supposed to feel when she got a supportive man on her side." She paused. "You know what, sis? I got shit to do. I'll talk to you later," she said before hanging up.

Damn, I can't believe she hung up on me. I didn't mean to judge the situation. I mean, yes, Adrian is wrong as hell for what he did and what he's been saying to her, but at the end of the day, that's who she chose to marry, and the best thing to do was to go home and work it out, not be out here running the streets with another nigga, and especially not start hanging out with Riley's hoe ass. I shook my head as I pulled up to Ollie's place.

Oliver

I was in the house, shaking my ass to trap music, when I heard my doorbell ring. I walked over to the door and checked the peephole. "Wassup, biiiiiiittttccchhh!" I yelled as I swung open the door. I could see the distraught look on her face, so I invited her in. "Girl, what's going on?" I asked as I turned the music down.

"When is the last time you talked to Lina?" she asked bluntly.

"Giiirrrrl, when she went off on us at the time clock," I said, rolling my eyes.

"So you hadn't really talked to her before then?" she asked.

"No, girl, why?" I asked, starting to get irritated.

"Well, listen to this," she started and then proceeded to tell me the entire story of Lina, Adrian, and Jaxon. Once she finished, I stood up and started doing a little hoe dance.

"Heeeeyyyy, Lina got her groove back! Lina got her groove back!" I sang, and she looked at me crazy. "What?" I asked as I stopped dancing.

"Are you OK with her sneaking around with another nigga?" I looked at her like she was crazy.

"Have you seen how happy she was this past week? You really thought that was Adrian's doing? Bitch, you crazy," I said with a laugh.

"But that's her husband!" she tried to reason with me.

"And? That don't mean he is her soulmate. Out of all the years we worked at that hospital, did that nigga ever send her flowers? Hell no. So shit, if a new nigga can make her happy and she ain't even popping the pussy for his ass, that's a blessing..." I paused, and she stared at me.

"Girl, it ain't even that deep. First of all, Adrian does not deserve Lina. Shit, rumor has it, his daddy hired some little hoe to be Adrian's side chick, so shit, we so worried about what Lina was doing that week, Adrian was probably getting his dick sucked," I said as I made a fellatio hand gesture.

"Wait. Where the hell you get that information from?" She gasped in surprised.

"From a nigga dick I was sucking that interns up there," I said, and she started laughing.

"Your ass is crazy," she said, wiping her tears.

"Bitch, I'm serious." I paused "So what did you say to Lina? Because clearly, you came over here with a different opinion," I said, trying to get to the real reason behind this visit.

"Well, she told me that I was too judgmental, and I told her that I wouldn't judge..." She paused, and I gave her the look. "I judged the shit out of her before I could even think, and she read me off and hung up." I looked at her and shook my head.

"What exactly did you say to her?" I asked, eager to hear her judgmental ass comments.

She sighed. "I can't believe you've been shacking up with another man, and you are married. How can you do that to Adrian?" I looked at her in shock. Even those words stung me.

"Girl, fuck Adrian, and let Lina live. That nigga ain't even trying to give her a baby yet, and she will be thirty in two years. She needs to move the fuck around and be with somebody that's right for her."

"Yeah, but they are married. Through the good and the bad, that's what they signed up for." I shook my head.

"For better or worse my ass. If you miserable with a motherfucker, don't continue to waste your one life just because you said some promises. Shit, niggas break promises every day, B!" I exclaimed as I quoted my favorite movie. "She found someone that brought her glow back. You telling me you want her to go back to the main nigga that stole it?" She sat there for a moment, and I could tell she was thinking over what I said.

"Damn, Ollie, you are right," she said in disbelief.

"Of course. I am a genius, you know," I said and popped my collar.

"But I ran into Adrian at the store today, and he seems like he might have changed." I gave her the *bitch, please* look. "You right. Fuck Adrian; we are Lina's friends," she said, and I laughed.

"Speaking of, you need to apologize to her for that comment. We are her friends, and we are on her team."

"You right, you right. Thanks, Ollie." I smiled, and she got up and started to head out.

Lina

The nerve of that heifer. She is supposed to be my friend, and she takin' this nigga side. I really can't believe her. I love Adrian, but I am not in love with him anymore. Hell, I'm starting to think I never was. I think I just loved the fact that he paid attention to me. I mean, I was shy, geeky, and a big lame. He was the big man on campus, and I just loved the fact that he chose me. Deep down, I knew that he wasn't for me. Hell, he wasn't even my type. I thought that I would grow to love him, but I just don't know.

I pulled up to the house, but I didn't want to go in. I pulled out my pre-rolled blunt, lit it, and took a puff. I cleared my mind and let the smoke fill me up. I closed my eyes and leaned back onto my seat, took another puff, and let my mind wander. I grabbed my phone, logged into Riley's account, and started lurking on the girl Hazel's profile. It did seem like she was taking jabs at me with her statuses. One read: **I know a chick who is about to lose her man because she would rather eat fried chicken than drink a smoothie.** I mean, damn. Clearly, if that wasn't about me, I didn't know what was. I took another puff and continued to scroll down. I mean, clearly, this bitch was obsessed with me. Another post read: **married women love playing the victim when their husbands finally tell them the truth.**

I wanted to get mad, but all I could do was laugh. *Shit, I am high as hell.* I continued to smoke and laugh at her posts. *Maaaannn, fuck this bitch. She can talk all this crap on the internet, but I bet she won't come through and—*

"Hold the fuck up," I said to myself as I clicked on a picture of her standing half naked in a mirror. I zoomed into the background. "That's my fucking bathroom!" *This motherfucker had this hoe ass trick in my motherfucking house, and she's half naked and shit. What the fuck? Calm down, Lina.* I started to do a breathing exercise to calm myself down.

I lit my blunt back up, got out of the car, and walked into the house. I could smell food cooking in the kitchen. I walked into the guest room and closed the door. I paced back and forth as I smoked. You know what? I'm not even mad at him. He's a nigga, and that's what niggas do. When we used to be in college, we would fight, and he would always find himself under a new chick. Fuck him and that bitch. I'm not mad at all. I mean, shit, I was just naked in the shower while Jaxon was pissing. So fuck it. I'm not mad, but I will beat that little bitch's ass when I see her. I finished my blunt, calmed myself down, and opened the door.

"Are you smoking weed?" Adrian asked as he stood in front of the door.

"Yeah, good looking, so what you got cooking? A bitch is hungrier than a motherfucker." I walked past him and into the kitchen. "Damn, this smells good, Adrian. Look at you. I leave for a week, and you become all domesticated and shit." I laughed and started to make a plate. "I ain't even gonna lie. I didn't even know your ass could cook. I guess when you gotta fend for yourself, you learn a lot of shit, huh?" I asked as I sat down at the table to eat.

"What's with all the foul language?" he asked as he made his plate.

"I'm high, nigga. I'm just saying shit," I said and started to laugh my ass off. He started laughing too.

"I can't even be mad at you, girl. I'm just happy you came home," he said with a smile.

"Mmmhmmm, I bet," I said dryly. We ate and talked for a bit, but I couldn't get my mind off him and that girl.

Chapter Six

Adrian (Monday Morning)

I sat at my desk, thinking about the weekend I had just spent with Lina. She spent most of it high, but that was OK because it took a lot of tension out of the room. We laughed, joked, and listened to music. It was like I was getting to know her again; the only thing that was strange was that she kept her distance. I could tell something was on her mind, but she wasn't trying to bring it up. She even slept in the guest room with the door locked. I knew it was going to take some time, but I was willing to win her back. I started to file through some papers when I heard a knock on the door.

"Come in," I said, and in walked Hazel. She closed the door and walked over to me.

"Hey, baby, I've missed you," she said as she rubbed my shoulders.

"Hazel, Lina and I are working it out, so what we had going on is over." I stood up, walked to the door, opened it, and gave her the *move around* look.

"Really, Adrian?" she asked as if she was surprised. I didn't say anything. She looked at me with anger and then stormed out. I sat at my desk with my head in my hands. *This shit is going to get messy; I know it,* I thought to myself as I finished filing the papers for this new account. I was about to order lunch when I heard a knock on my door. *I bet this ain't nobody but my damn dad.* "Come in," I said with a sigh.

Lina

I sat at my desk, but I couldn't get any work done. All I could think about was Adrian at the job with that lil' skank. I could feel myself getting angry as I scrolled through her page. I had been rereading these same statuses over and over again. This bitch was in love with my husband. I really wanted to beat this hoe's ass, but I knew that wouldn't hurt her. *I got it. I fucking got it.* I thought of the greatest plan.

I texted Riley and told her I was taking an early lunch. I ran out the building and headed home. When I got there, I ran upstairs and found this tight, short ass, red dress. I slipped it on and grabbed some black heels. I went downstairs and grabbed this big picnic basket out of the pantry. I looked in the mirror to make sure my hair was still cute; I had the braids pulled up into a big bun. I walked out the house, jumped in the car, and went to Adrian's favorite restaurant and ordered his favorite meal. I threw it in the basket and then drove to his job. When I pulled into the parking lot, I opened my sun visor and put on some lipstick. I stepped out of the car with the basket and walked into the building.

As soon as I hit the door, all eyes were on me. I walked in with my head high and my shoulders back like I owned the joint. I made my way toward Adrian's office. I could see Hazel staring at me from the corner of my eye. I turned to her, winked, and gave her the biggest smile. Then I knocked on Adrian's door. I could feel Hazel's eyes burning a hole in the back of my head, and all I could do was laugh as I walked into the office.

"Lina," Adrian said, surprised, as I locked the door.

"I brought you lunch," I said as I dropped the basket to the floor. I pulled the bobby pin out of my hair and let my braids fall messily down my back. I walked over to him, pulled his chair back from his desk, and straddled him, kissing him deeply in his mouth. He grabbed my ass and squeezed it.

"Damn, girl, you ain't got any panties on," he said through kisses. I smiled and unzipped his pants, pulling out his hard member. I rose up and then slid down on it. His office chair had a spring, which helped with the bounce. I could feel myself getting wetter and wetter as I watched his eyes roll into the back of his head. I grabbed him by his tie and slightly started to choke him.

"Yeah, motherfucker, take this pussy. Take this wet ass pussy, nigga," I moaned in his ear as I bounced harder and faster.

"Shit," he groaned. I let go of his tie and smacked him across the face.

"Lina, what the fuck," he said through clenched teeth.

"Shut the fuck up, and say my name," I said as I grabbed his neck.

"What?" he asked in pain and pleasure. I smacked him again.

"What's my fucking name!" I yelled, and he put his hand over my mouth.

"Girl, are you fucking crazy? Not so loud."

Him covering my mouth turned me on, and I started to slow grind back and forth on his dick, making sure to hit my G-spot. I grabbed him by his neck again and clenched my fingers around his throat.

"What's my motherfucking name?" I moaned as I started to ride his shit like it was the last dick in the world.

He groaned. "Lina!" he yelled out, and we both climaxed. I slowly stood up. I could feel his limp member slide out of me. I walked to the basket and grabbed some napkins out of the bag to cleaned myself up. I tossed a few napkins toward him and set the basket on the table.

"Enjoy your lunch, sweetie," I said as I fixed my dress and switched out of his office. All eyes were on me as I strutted out the door. I noticed Hazel looking the hardest, and I flipped my hair, smacking her in the face as I walked by. I got back to my car, ran home to change, and headed back to work. Seeing the look on that hoe's face was way better than beating her ass.

Hazel

Damn, I am missing Adrian's big dick invading my guts, I thought as I stapled some papers at my desk. I waited for the coast to be clear, and I went to his office. I knocked, and he let me in. I walked over to his desk and started to massage his shoulders, but he tensed up, and I could tell something was wrong.

"Hey, baby, I've missed you," I sang, trying to lighten the mood.

"Hazel, Lina and I are working it out, so what we had going on is over." He stood up, walked to the door, and opened it. I stared at him, a little hurt, but the look he gave me let me know that our little sexcapade was over.

"Really, Adrian?" I sputtered, but he didn't reply. I could feel my anger level rising as I stormed out of his office and into the bathroom to calm myself down. *I can't believe that motherfucker. How the fuck can he do me like that? I got something for his goofy ass. Just wait and see.* I looked at myself in the mirror and started to breathe. *Relax, Hazel. You got this,* I thought as I gathered myself and walked out of the bathroom. As soon as I rounded the corner, I saw Lina walking in with a tight, short ass dress that was too damn small for her big-body ass. She was carrying a picnic basket and was headed right to Adrian's office.

So that was why his punk ass kicked me out the office? He must have known she was coming by. I stared at her as she walked past, trying to figure out what she had that I didn't. I guessed she caught me staring because she turned to me, winked, and gave me the biggest smile. For a moment, if I didn't know any better, I could have sworn she knew who I was. I watched as she knocked and then walked into Adrian's office, closing the door behind her.

"God damn, Lina ass is looking good as fuck in that damn dress," Aaron cooed.

"I know, right? All that thick ass booty. Adrian know he can't handle all of that," Nate replied, and they both dapped.

"Well, honestly, I think her fat ass needs to get on Weight Watchers because she's clearly overweight," I butted in, and they both looked at me and then started to laugh uncontrollably.

"First of all, Hazel, Lina looks like yes, and you look like no," Nate joked, and Aaron started to laugh again. "Also, you might need to get some pointers from Lina. I remember how you almost burned your apartment down trying to boil water," Nate joked, and Aaron started to laugh again.

"Fuck both of you, and fuck that ugly heifer too," I hissed.

"Well, it sounds like Adrian has that covered," Aaron said as he walked closer to Adrian's office door, and I followed.

"What's my motherfucking name!" we heard Lina yell.

"Damn, Lina a freak. She up in there handling ya boy," Aaron said as he nudged me on the arm.

"Lina!" I heard Adrian yell, and my heart sank. I walked away from the office door and started heading toward the exit. I stopped when I heard his office door open. Lina walked out, and her hair was down, and her dress was a little bunched. I wanted to run up and choke the shit out of her, but I stood there, frozen. She walked past me and flipped her hair, and her braids slightly smacked me in the face. She walked out of the building, and I stood there with the boo boo face. I looked at Aaron, and he was smirking. I stormed over to him, grabbed him by his tie, and dragged him into his office.

"I am going to kill that lil' hoe! Can you believe that bitch hit me in the face with her stank ass braids" I raged after closing the door.

"Yeah, she did do that shit. Now when I see it happen to someone else, ima say they just got hazeled!" He said and let out a loud chuckle. I looked at him and rolled my eyes. "Wipe your face. Your jealousy is showing," Aaron said, and it pissed me off.

"You know what, Aaron? Stop being a fucking asshole!" I sneered.

"How am I an asshole? You are the one that's fuming because a married couple had sex," he mocked. I started to pace the room. He continued to talk, but I tuned him out. I couldn't believe that he was just in there having sex with her, knowing that I was here in the building. How the fuck could he do this to me? We were supposed to be in love. We were supposed to be getting married! *I have to get that trick out of the picture, or I swear to God I am going to snap.*

"You know what, Aaron? You are taking too long to come up with a plan. I will come up with one on my own." I huffed angrily.

"Hazel, I really don't understand your obsession with

Adrian. I mean, damn, is the dick really that good that you are willing to plot on a woman that doesn't even know you exist?" he snapped, and I could tell he was getting agitated.

"You don't understand, because you are basic," I muttered.

"Bitch, yo' hoe ass is basic. You are in my office, remember?" he said and opened the door. "In the words of Martin: get to steppin'."

I walked to the door and closed it back.

"I need your help, Aaron. What do I have to do to get it?" I asked, and he walked over to his desk and leaned against it so that his hips protruded out.

"Well," he said as he looked down. "How about you show me what that mouth do?" I stared at him, hoping he was joking, but he wasn't.

"For real?" I asked.

"Yeah. Come swallow this motherfucker," he said as he undid his belt buckle. I rolled my eyes and walked over to him. I got on my knees as he pulled it out. I was shocked, he actually had a nice sized package. I opened my mouth and let his dick fill it. I sucked lazily, hoping that he would just cum like a lame little virgin ass nigga. He moaned and groaned, and it kind of turned me on, so I sucked faster, making sure I was slobbing it down and getting it nice and wet.

"Damn, girl," he moaned as his knees started to buckle. He grabbed my head, and I held on to his hips. "Don't stop. I'm about to nut," he said, and I tried to pull back, but he pushed my head and started to stroke back and forth. The next thing I knew, he was filling my mouth up with his bitter ass nut. He finally let my head go, and I quickly ran to the garbage can to spit.

"So do we have a deal now?" I asked as I headed to the door.

"Hell yeah, girl. I am yours for the taking," he joked, and I walked out of his office and headed to the bathroom. I went to the sink and rinsed the taste of his nut out of my mouth. I stared at myself in the mirror. *What the hell are you doing, Hazel? This is not you. Is it really that damn serious?* My mind raced as I tried to justify my actions and the actions to come. I am doing this for my family. Once I marry him and we put our money together, we can really boss up and do some real ass shit. We won't have to work for his dad; we can open up a husband and wife tag-team firm. I wiped my mouth, fixed my makeup, and walked back to my desk. I had to think of a plan, and I had to think of one quick.

Jaxon (Wednesday evening)

I walked into the bar after work, hoping to run into Lina. I sat on the barstool and ordered a beer. "Hey, where's Jo?" I asked when the bartender brought me my drink.

"She's off today. She'll be back Friday night," she said and continued to make drinks. The bar was pretty dead. There were a few people scattered around at the tables, eating and talking. None were on the dance floor, but the DJ was still spinning. I walked over to one of the booths, sat down, and drank some of the beer.

I pulled out my phone and started to scroll through pictures of Lina and me when we went to the carnival. I still can't believe that out of all the time we spent together, we never kissed. I regret not seizing the moment when I had a chance. I missed her little thick, sexy self so much. Part of me wanted to just show up to her crib with a radio blasting *All I Do Is Think of You*, but I'm not trying to mess up what she has going on, but damn, I nee—my thoughts were interrupted by this couple behind me. It sounded as if they were plotting on some girl.

"We are going to trick her here, and then I'm going to put something in her drink," the guy said.

"Yeah, then I'll be waiting outside, and we will take her to the hotel across the street and…" She continued to talk, but I didn't want to listen to that shit. I left some money on the table for the beer, got up, and left the bar. I walked to my car and headed out.

Adrian

I walked into the house. "Baby, are you here?" I called out, but I didn't get an answer. I walked into the kitchen, and there was food on the stove. Things were a little better the last few days, especially after Lina surprised me at the office with lunch. I got turned on, just thinking about how she came in my office and fucked the hell out of me. I mean, I had to get an earful from my dad, but shit, the love from my wife was worth it.

I thought we were starting to get back to normal. I lifted the pot and sniffed the savory aroma. *Damn, this girl knows what she's doing in this damn kitchen.* I put the lid back on and went searching for my baby. I walked into the room, and her work clothes were scattered on the floor. She was in the bed, wrapped in a towel, sleeping. *Damn, she is so beautiful.* I walked over to her and trailed my fingers up her leg, softly caressing her thigh. I could feel my third leg start to grow.

"Jaxon," she moaned softly in her sleep. I quickly drew back my hand. I didn't know what to think. Who the fuck was Jaxon, and why the fuck was she moaning his name in her sleep? I searched around the room, trying to find her phone. I grabbed it from the nightstand and pressed the home button. *What the hell? When the fuck did she start locking her phone?* I thought as an uneasy feeling crept across my stomach.

"I think I'm going to be sick," I groaned as I tried every

possible code—her birthday, my birthday, everything—until I was locked out of her phone. I walked downstairs and started to pace the living room.

"Is she cheating on me?" I asked myself quietly. "Naw, she can't be—not after the way she fucked me in my office. Her shit was nice and tight. Ain't nobody been in there but me, right?" I tried to reassure myself. I held my stomach. It was all in knots.

"Hey, are you OK?" I heard Lina's voice behind me, startled, I quickly spun around.

"Yeah, I'm fine. I was just trying to call my phone with your phone, but I didn't know the code," I said as I held up her phone in my hand.

"It's your name, bae," she nonchalantly said as she walked into the kitchen. "Did you eat, bae!" she yelled back, and I could hear her taking plates out of the cabinet.

"No, not yet," I replied as I put in the password and went right to her messages. *No messages from a nigga name Jaxon or anything.* The only thing I saw were hella messages from Riley. I opened the messages just to see what they were talking about.

Riley: Girl I am still laughing about the look you said Hazel had on her face when you walked out the office (laughing emoji)

Lina: Girl that look was all I needed, let her run and post that (laughing with tears emoji)

Riley: You think her and Adrian had something going on (thinking emoji)

Lina: Girl don't know and too damn tired to give a fuck (Girl shrugging emoji)

Riley: Have you talked to Jaxon

That was the last message. I stood there, frozen. I clicked out of the messages and threw the phone on the couch. *What the hell is going on? How did she find out about Hazel?* My mind was whirling with questions. I felt like I had just opened the chamber of secrets.

"Hey, you good?" Lina walked out of the kitchen with her plate and sat on the couch and turned the TV on. "Your plate is made and, on the counter," she said as she started to eat.

"OK, cool. Thanks, baby," I said and walked into the kitchen. I wanted to confront her about this other nigga, but shit, I can't bring his ass up, knowing that she knows about Hazel. *How the fuck does she even know about Hazel?* I grabbed my phone out of my pocket and went to Hazel's page. I wasn't really into this social media shit, but Lina was talking about Hazel posting, so I had to check it out. I scrolled through her page, and I could see she was posting crazy ass shit, but the thing that stood out the most was a picture that she posted. *That's my damn bathroom.* What the fuck, man? Women these days don't know how to be discreet, gotta post every fucking thing. Damn, if Lina saw this shit, there's no telling who else had. I have to play this shit cool. I mean, shit. We are here, and we are back together. She ain't said shit about it, and I'm not going to either. We are just going to work this relationship out.

I grabbed my plate and walked out to join Lina. She was watching *Martin*. I sat next to her, but I would be lying if I said this didn't feel awkward as hell. I couldn't get the thought out of my mind that she was with another man. I was angry and even angrier that I had to hold this shit in. I couldn't even enjoy my food. I looked at Lina. She was laughing at the show and eating her food like nothing was going on. *Did she fuck me just to spite Hazel?* My head was starting to hurt, and my stomach was turning. *What the fuck is going on, man?*

Lina (Friday Morning)

I sat at my desk, looking down at my phone, contemplating on if I should text Jaxon or not. It had been rounding two weeks, and I hadn't heard from him. I'd wanted to call, but I just didn't know what to say. I kept writing, erasing, writing, and erasing messages, but there was nothing I could think of. I'd been trying to live this life with Adrian, but it really wasn't what I wanted anymore. I mean, I only fucked him because I wanted to see the shitty look on that girl's face.

"Hey, Lina," I heard a voice behind me. I turned around and saw Sam standing there. I rolled my eyes and turned back to my phone. "Really, bitch?" she said, and I couldn't hold my composure and started laughing.

"What? Too dramatic?" I asked as I turned around. Sam was one of my best friends. Yeah, we argued and might not agree, but she was my bitch for life.

"Girl, I came in here with a whole apology, and you are ruining the moment," she said with a serious face.

"OK, proceed."

She paused and then took a deep breath. "Look, Lina. I am sorry about how I reacted when you told me about your situation with Adrian. You deserve to be happy, and sometimes, marriages don't work..." She paused. "But whatever you decide to do, I will be behind you 1,000 percent."

I smiled, stood up, and gave her a hug. "Thank you, sis." I heard my text notification go off, and I grabbed my phone. "It's

Adrian. He wants to meet up at the bar tonight to talk…" I paused. "What the hell does he want to talk about at a bar?" I looked at Sam.

"Maybe he's going to show you the man you are looking for. Are you going to head up there?" she asked as she sat at the desk. I gave her the *yeah, right* look

"I don't know, man. I mean, I love Adrian, and I think we would be really great friends, but he's just not what I want, and don't I deserve to be happy? I mean, hell, I'm ready to have kids, and he keep telling me to wait. Bitch, I am damn near thirty. I deserve to have the life I fucking want. Shit, I only have one," I said as I plopped down in my chair and put my head in my hands.

"You do, sis, but I still think you should hear him out," she said sternly.

"OK, I'll meet up with him, but I am going to tell him about Jaxon, and whatever happens after that, I will deal with it." I grabbed the phone and texted him back and continued with my day.

I got off work and headed home. Adrian said he wanted to meet around seven, so I had a little time to shower and change clothes. *Adrian, I met a guy, and I really think we should part ways.* I practiced the words in my head as I pulled my jeans up and pulled my shirt over my head. *Look, bae, I love you, but I think I might be in love with someone else.* I shook my head no. That would break his heart. I looked at the clock, and it was six thirty. I slipped on my shoes and ran out of the house. I pulled up to the bar at exactly seven. I walked inside and looked around. I didn't see Adrian. *Good. I am glad I'm here first; it gives me a chance to drink and get some liquid courage.*

"Hey, Jo, give me my usual," I said, and she started making my drink.

"Where's Jaxon?" she asked, and I shrugged.

"We are kind of not talking right now," I said as she handed me the drink. "Oh, so that's why he be in here looking like a home-sick puppy." She placed a napkin next to my glass and went to tend to her other customers. I sat, sipping my drink and waiting for Adrian to show up. *I hope he is not going to stand me up like last time.* I ordered another drink and looked at my phone. It was seven thirty.

"Hey, Lina," I heard a familiar voice behind me. I turned around and saw Aaron standing there with a silly grin on his face.

"Hey, Aaron, how are you?" I asked as he sat next to me.

"I'm doing good. Adrian sent me here to let you know that he cracked his phone and had to run to the Apple store, but he will be here," he said, and he waved Jo over to order a drink. I rolled my eyes and finished my drink.

"I'll just meet him at home," I said as I started to stand up.

Aaron

"Hold on, Lina. Don't leave me here all by myself after I've come all this way to deliver this message. You can at least have a drink with me," I said, trying to convince her to stay.

"You lucky it's Friday," she said as she sat back down.

"Cool, cool. Bartender, let me get a beer and another drink for this lovely lady." I looked at Lina. "Hey, I don't want to embarrass you, but you're looking pretty good over there." I flirted and she smiled. I smiled back and suddenly I felt like we were back in college. *Damn, she's so fine.* I swear I'm starting to have second thoughts. She's a good ass woman, and she really doesn't deserve any of this shit. I was pulled out of my thoughts by my phone going off. It was a text from Hazel

Hazel: Don't flake out now nigga

Me: I'm not

I put the phone down and tried not to meet the evil glare that I knew Hazel was giving me from across the room. I looked back at Lina. "Hey, boo. You have some lipstick on your teeth," I lied, hoping it would make her go to the bathroom.

"Oh my God, really? I'm going to run to the bathroom. Watch my drink," she said as she got up and walked into the direction of the bathroom. I watched her as she disappeared into the crowd. I looked around to make sure no one was looking, and then I slipped a roofie into her drink. My phone went off again, and it was Hazel

Hazel: Good boy step one is complete

I placed my phone down and took a drink from my beer. *This ain't me, man.* This ain't what I should be doing to get some damn pussy. Shit, I get pussy. *Man, I don't need this karma in my life.* I was about to knock over her drink, but Lina grabbed it and started to drink.

"Hey, slow down, girl," I said, trying to grab the drink, but it was too late. *Fuck it, man. The plan must go on.* "Bartender, one more drink, two shots, and a beer." Lina looked at me.

"Are you trying to get me drunk, Aaron?" she joked. I laughed.

"Of course not. I'm just trying to show you a good time. I know things with you and AJ been on the fritz, I figured you needed some fun before he comes in being a downer." She laughed.

"Well, cheers to that," she said, and we both clinked our glass together and took the shots.

"You know what, Aaron? I've always like you," Lina chatted as I drank my beer.

"Really?" I asked with a smile.

"Yes, you were always such a great friend to Adrian. He would always tell me that if he wanted real advice, you were the one to give it," she assured, and I smiled. "Just know that out of all his friends, I appreciate you the most. I mean, just look. You drove all the way out here just to do him a favor. You are a great friend," she praised, and I instantly started to feel like a total jackass.

"Well, thank you, Lina," I said as I gulped down the rest of my beer and put my one finger up to order another. "You know I always liked you as well. I was going to shoot my shot in college, but AJ got to you first." I chuckled. I could feel the buzz from the liquor.

"Can I ask you a question?" She paused. "But you have to promise to tell me the truth," she added.

"Sure. What's on your mind?" I inquired.

"How long has Adrian been fucking that duck looking bitch that works at the office?" she questioned, and I choked on my drink.

"Damn, you knew about that?" I spoke hesitantly.

"I mean, I wasn't really sure, but thanks for clearing that up for me," she murmured, and I could feel her heart breaking.

"I'm sorry, Lina. I—" I started, but she cut me off.

"Fuck it. Jo, hit me with another one," she slurred.

Chapter Seven

Lina

I sat with my head down at the bar. "Are you OK, Lina?" I heard Jo ask, and I lifted my head to see her, but it felt so heavy.

"Yeah, she's OK. I am a friend of her husband's, and I am going to take her home," I heard Aaron say as he grabbed me and pulled me off the stool. I stumbled along beside him until we were met with the cool night air.

"Thanks, Aaron, but I got it from here," I slurred as I pulled away to walk toward my car.

"I don't think so, Lina," I heard a woman's voice. I tried to turn around, but I was hit in the head, and before I knew it, I was out like a light.

Jo

I watched as the guy pulled Lina out of the bar, and seconds later, a woman followed up behind them. *Something doesn't sit right with me. I've watched her drink here many of times, and not once has she even acted like that. If I didn't know any better, I would have thought she was drugged.* I ran to the door to see if they were in the parking lot, but it was empty. I looked across the street, and I could see the woman that ran out of here get out of her car and walk into the hotel. I pulled out my phone to call Jaxon.

"Hello?" He picked up on the first ring. "Wassup, Jo? I'm pulling up in like five minutes."

"Jaxon, something is going on with Lina—"

He cut me off. "What you mean? Something like what?" he asked.

"I think this couple drugged her and took her to this hotel across the street from the bar," I said in a panic.

"I'm on the way, Jo."

Lina

I was awakened by a strong sting across my face. "Wake up, bitch!" I heard a woman's voice yell. I opened my eyes, and the room was dim, and my sight was blurry, and my head was pounding. I felt as if I had been hit in the head with a bag of bricks.

"What the hell is going on?" I sat up on the bed and blinked several times. I looked around the room, trying to assess the situation. I blinked a few more times, finally getting a clear image of Hazel and Aaron.

"You are about to get yours, hoe," Hazel said as she slapped me again. I tried to get up, but I felt dizzy. I had no control over my body. *How in the hell did I get myself in this situation, and why do I feel so damn out of control of myself?* My questions swirled in my head as I looked back and forth from Hazel to Aaron.

"What do you want from me?" I slurred in confusion. She walked over to me with her phone in her hand.

"Watch this," she said as she pressed play, and it was a video of me with my pants down as Aaron thrust on top of me. *I can't believe what I am seeing. I don't remember any of this. I think I am going to be sick,* I thought as I began to gag.

"Wait, did you rape me!" I yelled as I looked at Aaron. I could feel the tears welling up in my eyes.

"No, silly. This is just staged to make it look like you guys were having sex. He was too scared to actually do it." She sneered in his direction. "But as you can see, we made it look as if you were actually enjoying it. That makes it a lot better." I stared at the video. My legs were wrapped around him, and my arms were around his neck.

"Man, I need some air," Aaron said and walked out of the room. I was overwhelmed, and the room started to fade to black. I was awakened again by her slapping me in the face.

"Hold on, bitch. I'm not done yet," she said as she scrolled to another video. "This video right here is real," she said as she showed me a video of her and Adrian fucking. I turned away, but she grabbed me by my chin and made me watch. "We've been fucking every day since you left the house, and that damn dick is good as fuck, sis." She laughed. "Once I show Adrian this video of you and Aaron, he will disown you, and I will replace you." She let out a sinister laugh.

"Bitch, you sound stupid as hell. You do know that, right?" I jeered. "I mean, really damn stupid. Adrian ain't gonna fall for this stupid ass video!" I yelled, and she smacked me again.

"He's going to believe it just like you almost did." She chuckled. "Did you rape me?" she mocked. "Shit, you are the stupid one to think Aaron was your friend." She laughed again.

Visions from the bar flashed through my head. I remembered drinking and laughing with Aaron, and not once did I have the feeling that he was setting me up.

"You do know once I get out of here, I am going to fuck you up, right?" I threatened.

"That's *if* you get out of this." She got right in my face and emphasized the word *if.* The tone in her voice scared me. *Is the bitch trying to say she's going to kill me? Come on, Lina. You have to fight through whatever the fuck is going on with your body.* I slapped Hazel in the face, grabbed her by her hair, and slammed her head down into the nightstand that was next to the bed. She stumbled back and fell on the floor. I pulled myself up and awkwardly stumbled to the door. I pulled it open and looked down the hall. Aaron was standing at the end of the hall entrance, with his back to me. I could hear him talking on the phone. Down the opposite hall was a wall. *Damn it, where can I go?* I thought as I looked forward. *Thank you, God.* I praised as I noticed a stair exit. I quickly darted across the hall and out the door. I suddenly felt weak as I staggered up the stairs. I could hear Aaron as he called Hazel's name. I moved faster until I reached the top. I pushed open the door, and I was on the roof.

Jaxon

I pulled up to the bar, and Jo and I ran across the street to the hotel. "Hey, did a guy walk in here with a girl that was really drunk?" I quickly asked the clerk behind the desk.

"If I had a dollar for every time someone asked me that," he said nonchalantly as he flipped through a magazine. I snatched the magazine out of his hands.

"Motherfucker, this is serious!" I yelled.

"Man, I don't know. I've been in the backroom, watching the game." He shrugged. "No one rang the bell." I angrily threw the magazine at his face and stormed out of the hotel with Jo hot on my tail. *Man, what the fuck is going on? I swear if that motherfucker hurts my girl, I am going to have to put his ass six feet under.* My mind suddenly remembered the two people in the bar plotting, and I realized they had been plotting on Lina this entire time, and I ignored it.

"What are we going to do? She could be in trouble," she said as we walked back to my car.

"I'm going to try and call her," I said as I pulled out my phone.

"This shit is fucking crazy. I should have known..." She paused and grabbed me by my shoulder. "Jaxon, the roof." She pointed. I turned around, and I could see Lina. I ran back to the hotel.

Lina

I stood on the roof, looking down at the world below me. Blurred lights speeding by made me dizzy. I looked forward and closed my eyes as the cool night air brushed my face. I held my head between my hands; I could feel myself unsteadily stumbling forward. *Why am I feeling so impaired?* was the only question running through my mind as I held on to the ledge. I only had a few drinks, and they were pretty watered down. I opened my eyes, staring down, and the swirling lights continued to make me feel lightheaded. I turned around and perched myself slightly on the ledge, just enough to where I could rest but still keep my feet on the ground.

"Lina!" I heard a voice yell loudly, startling me so much that I lost my balance. Suddenly, I felt like a lightweight. *I'm falling.* I felt a strong pair of arms around me, pulling me back from my near-death experience.

"Hey, girl, are you OK?" Aaron asked as I fell to the ground.

"Get off me!" I yelled as I kicked him in the nuts.

"Bitch!" I heard Hazel scream as she ran toward me. She jumped on top of me, punching me in the face. I grabbed her by her hair, pulling her down as I rolled on top of her. I punched her in her nose twice. We rolled back and forth, hitting each other in the nose, eyes, and mouth. I was in so much pain, but I wasn't going to stop until this bitch was dead. I was on top again. I grabbed Hazel by her hair and was getting ready to slam her head into the pavement.

"Lina!" I heard two voices call out. I looked back, and both Jaxon and Adrian were standing there, looking at each other. I was so busy looking at them that I let Hazel get off a sucker punch. I fell over and rolled on my back. She must have been tired as well because she just laid there.

I looked over at her, and I prayed that I didn't look as bad as she did. "Bitch, if you wanted Adrian that bad, you could have just said so." I took the last bit of energy I had to knock her ass out.

"Aw shit, this fight is going on WorldStar!" the hotel clerk yelled as he held up his phone.

"Get the fuck outta here before I fuck you up!" I heard Jaxon yell.

"Ight, man, chill," the clerk said and then left.

"Come on, baby," I heard Jaxon say as he picked me up.

"Hold on, nigga! That's my wife!" Adrian yelled out as he ran over to me.

"Adrian, your fucking side chick over there drugged me and had your buddy pretend to rape me, all because she wanted you to herself. At this point, she can have you," I said as I grabbed Jaxon's hand and headed toward the door.

"Congratulations, nigga. You played yourself," Jaxon said as he picked me up and carried me down the stairs. "I'm going to take you to the hospital, baby. I think you might have a broken face." He smiled. I wanted to laugh, but my face might fall the fuck off. I just closed my eyes and laid my head on his chest.

Adrian

I watched as my wife got carried away by who I assumed was Jaxon. I walked over to Aaron. "Nigga, what the fuck is going on?" I asked in anger.

"Listen, man. Hazel came up with this plan to drug Lina and have me pretend to have sex with her, but I couldn't go through with that shit, so I called you." I looked at him like he had lost his mind, and then I knocked his ass out. I walked up to Hazel as she laid unconscious on the ground. I can't believe this bitch had the fucking balls to do this shit. I mean, I can't lie. She's really a ride or die, but I'm not into that crazy ass shit. I heard her phone going off. I grabbed and picked it up.

"Hey, is the deed done?" I hung up quickly. I knew that voice from anywhere. *I should have known my dad was behind this goofy ass shit; these two fools ain't conniving enough to come up with this type of plan.* I dropped her phone and headed toward the door. I walked down the stairs and told the clerk to call the ambulance for the dummies on the roof; then I went to find my dad.

Lina (Saturday morning)

I lay in the hospital bed with a busted nose, busted lip, and swollen eyes with busted blood vessels; I looked like something out of the walking dead. The pain medicine was working for my physical pain, but emotionally, I was fucked up. *I can't believe this.* I'm lying in the hospital because my husband is clearly out here slanging good dick and fucking bitch's brains up. I mean, these motherfuckers really drugged me. Like, really, who does that? I opened my eyes. Jaxon was sitting in the chair, watching TV. I shifted in the bed, and he turned toward me.

"Hey, sleepy head, how are you feeling?" he asked as he ran his hands through my hair.

"Like I've been hit by a truck." I tried to laugh, but it hurt. There was a knock on the door, and in walked Ollie, Sam, and Riley.

"Good morning, Laila Ali," Ollie joked as he kissed me on top of my head.

"Girl, you are viral," Riley said with a laugh.

"What you mean, viral?" I winced.

"Girl, as in you are all over the internet, knocking a bitch out," Sam added as she pulled up the video.

"Well, I'll be damned," I said as I watched my and Hazel's brawl on the phone.

"This the best part right here. Bitch, if you wanted Adrian

that bad, you could have just said so. *Bow*! Knocked the thought out of that bitch," Ollie said as he punched the air.

"Who uploaded the video?" I asked.

"You don't remember the hotel clerk on the roof with us?" Jaxon chimed in.

"Shit, I damn near don't remember anything. I think I was roofied or something," I said, and Jaxon shook his head.

"Yeah, that's what Jo thought. She called me because she was worried."

"Damn, remind me to send her a thank you basket because she is the real MVP," I said as I sat up slightly in the bed. I heard another knock on the door, and in walked Adrian. Jaxon stood up, ready to attack.

"Hey, he's good. He didn't know about the setup, Jaxon." I reached out and grabbed him back.

"Can I please have a word with my wife?" he asked, and everyone looked at me.

"It's OK, you guys," I said as they all got up and headed toward the door.

"I'll be right outside the door, shorty," Jaxon said as he kissed me on my forehead. I could see Adrian clenching his fists. Jaxon walked past him and left out the room.

"Damn, Lina, that's what you on?" he asked in an abrasive tone.

"First of all, Adrian, Hazel showed me a video of you and her fucking, so please don't even step to me like that. She also told me that you have been fucking her every day since I left; me and Jaxon haven't even kissed," I said, trying to roll my eyes. He just looked away. "Exactly, and now I am laid up in a fucking hospital bed because you couldn't keep your motherfucking dick in your pants for one fucking week!" I yelled in anger.

"I'm sorry, Lina," he said, and I could tell he was sincere.

"It's cool, Adrian. This just shows me that we are not meant to be together. We can still be friends, but when I leave out of here, I am going to file for divorce. I want to be happy, and I would be lying to myself if I believed that I will be happy with you," I said, not trying to sound harsh, but I knew it came off as such.

"You right," he said, and it took me by surprise. "You deserve happiness, and I can't give you that, because I am not happy with myself. There is no way I can make you happy. All you've ever done was be a good wife to me, and I betrayed, belittled, and treated you less than how you should have been treated. I just want you to know that I am truly sorry, and I wish you the best." He walked over to me and kissed me on my swollen lips. "Keep in touch, baby girl," he said and just walked out of the room. I instantly felt my stomach drop. *Is this really what I want? Am I really going to leave my husband?* Thoughts swirled through my head as the door opened back up and the crew walked in.

"You good?" Sam asked as she walked over to grab my hand.

"Yes, I'm OK." I could feel the tears starting to well up in my eyes. "I'm just ready for all of this to be over. I'm tired, you guys," I said, turning my back to them and facing the wall.

"OK, boo," Riley said.

"We know shit is crazy. We will be back to check on you later," Ollie added. They all said they loved me and left out of the room.

"Shorty." Jaxon rubbed my back. "I know shit is crazy now, but just know I got you." I rolled over and looked at him. I could see the sincerity in his eyes. "I really think it was God's plan that we met. I truly believe that you are my rib," he said, and I instantly started crying.

"Where have you been all my life?" I asked.

"Shit, looking for you."

"You are so corny," I joked, and he laughed.

"Yeah, I know," he said with a smile. There was a knock on the door, and the nurse walked in to check on me.

"Hey, sweetie. How's your pain?" she asked as she started to check my vitals.

"Honestly, my entire body feels as if I was hit by a truck," I groaned.

"Well, I do have a few medications for you to take that are going to help with the pain. Do you need something to help you sleep?" she asked as she scanned my bracelet.

"Yes, please," I replied, hoping that I could just go to sleep and wake up from this long ass nightmare. She smiled as she popped the pills out of their foil packages. She handed them to me with a cup of water. I put the all into my mouth and flushed them down. She gathered up her machine and headed toward the door.

"Page me if you need me, Mrs. Long," she said and closed the door behind her. I looked at Jaxon, and he was sitting back in the chair with his eyes closed. I laid back and gazed out of the window; the sun was shining, and it seemed like a nice day. I could feel the medicine kicking in, and I closed my eyes and drifted off to sleep.

Adrian

I walked into the hospital and up to the front desk. "Hey, good morning. I am looking for my wife, Darlina Long," I said to the receptionist. "Yes, Mrs. Long is upstairs in room 305; just make a left at the gift shop, and you will see the elevators. Once there, you can ask someone at the nurse's station to direct you to the room," she said as she gave me a visitor's pass. I thanked her and headed toward the elevators. I got upstairs and stood in front of her door. I could hear voices from inside. I took a deep breath, knocked on the door, and walked inside, and all eyes were on me. Jaxon stood up, and I was ready to knock his ass the fuck out.

"Can, I please have a word with my wife?" I asked, and everyone looked at Lina. She assured them that everything would be OK, and they all exited out of the room but not before Jaxon kissed Lina on the forehead.

"Damn, Lina, that's what you on?" I asked, angry at the fact she had a new nigga trying to fight her battles.

I could see the anger rise in her face as she told me about Hazel's video of us. I instantly felt ashamed and I couldn't help but look away as she yelled. I felt stupid for even being here. All of this was my fucking fault. I started this affair with Hazel, not knowing what kind of crazy can of worms I was opening. I looked back at Lina. Her face was bruised, but her beauty still shined through. She didn't deserve to be lying in a hospital bed. *I'm the reason she is here, and because of that, I know that I don't deserve her.*

"Exactly, and now I am laid up in a fucking hospital bed because you couldn't keep your motherfucking dick in your pants for one fucking week!" she yelled in anger.

"I'm sorry, Lina." My voice was low, and I almost didn't recognize it. She started to say that we were not meant to be together and that she wanted a divorce, and I felt my stomach drop. My mouth became dry, and my head started to slowly spin.

"I want to be happy, and I would be lying to myself if I believed that I will be happy with you." Those words cut like a knife. I didn't know what to say.

"You're right," I heard myself say. I continued to tell her that she deserved better, and I couldn't give her that because I wasn't happy with myself. I was praying that if she heard those words, she would take pity on me and give me another chance to make this right. But as I listened to my words, I realized that I didn't deserve her pity. I didn't deserve her kindness, and I damn sure didn't deserve her love. I walked over to her and kissed her on the lips. "Keep in touch, baby girl," was all I could say as I turned and headed toward the door. I wanted her to call out and stop me, but she didn't. I walked out with my head down and headed toward the elevators.

"Can you believe both women from that viral fight are here?" I couldn't help but overhear the nurses gossiping at the desk. I walked over to them.

"Hey, can you tell me what room Hazel Watson is in?" I questioned.

"Yes, she is in room 320," she replied as she pointed toward the opposite direction from Lina's room. I thanked her and headed down the hall. I knocked and then entered.

"Adrian, what-what are you doing here?" she stammered, and I could hear the fear in her voice.

"Hazel, what the fuck were you thinking, attacking my fucking wife like that? Are you fucking sick in the head or something!" I roared, and I could see the fear in her eyes.

"I'm sorry, Adrian. It wasn't supposed to go that far. I love you, and I just wanted to be with you—" I cut her off.

"Love? Are you kidding me? Please tell me that you are joking. We were only fucking for what? A week or two? So please miss me with that love bullshit." I scoffed.

"I've always loved you. Why do you think I came back?" she cried out. "Your dad told me that you wanted me here and that you were trapped in a relationship that you hated. I dropped everything to be here for you, and then I get here, and you pretend to be unhappy just to fuck me and then toss me to the side. So yes, after that shit, I was fucking angry, and I let the fucking anger get the best of me. Am I proud of it? Hell fucking no, but I can't change shit now." She stopped, and I could see the tears flowing down her face. I looked in her eyes, and I didn't see a crazy woman. I saw a broken woman that was just doing what she thought she had to do to get love.

"Because of you, my fucking wife is in the arms of another man. You could have probably had me if you didn't pull that stunt, but now, I don't want anything to do with your evil, vindictive, selfish, crazy ass. And I hope Lina find you and beat your ass some fucking more." I turned and stormed out of the room.

"Adrian! Adrian, come back here! Don't you fucking leave me!" she yelled as the door closed behind me. I stood outside the door, trying to calm my nerves. How in the hell did I fuck all this shit up? I walked back to the elevator. Lina's friends were standing at the nurses' station, talking. I stood back, but Sam noticed me. Her gaze met mine, and I could see the sorrow in her eyes. She shook her head and turned back to their conversation. The elevator opened, and they got on. I waited until it closed and then went to get on the next one. I walked out of the hospital, sad and alone.

Chapter Eight

Lina

"Hold on, bitch! I ain't done yet!" Hazel screamed.

I woke up in a cold sweat, holding my chest as I looked around the room. "It was just a dream, girl," I assured myself as I caught my breath. The room was dark other than the little light that shone from the TV. I looked around, and the room was empty. I grabbed my phone to check my messages.

Jaxon: Hey baby I ran out to get something to eat, I will be back shortly

I clicked out of Jaxon's message and saw one from Adrian, so I opened it.

Adrian: Lina please give me another chance; I love you and I don't think I can live without you

I put the phone down, and I could feel the tears running down my face. *Lord, why am I in this situation?* Why couldn't my husband just love me for me? All of this happened because he couldn't accept the fact that I was fucking changing. People fucking change, man, and instead of him trying to work with me, he chose to work against me and brought that psycho ass bitch into our lives.

Wiping my eyes, I grabbed my phone again. I started to go through pictures of when Adrian and I were happy. Because, yes, at one point, we were completely happy. I sobbed silently, reminiscing about the past and how great it used to be.

Adrian

"How can you mend a broken heart? How can you stop the rain from falling down?" Al Green sang in the background as I drank carelessly from a bottle of Henny. "How can you mend this broken man? Yeah, how can a loser ever win?" I slurred out of tune. "Yeah, sing it, Al," I cried out loud as I grabbed my phone and started to go through old pictures of Lina and me. She was so beautiful, with such a precious soul, and I fucking lost her to another fucking man. I switched over to the text messages.

Me: Lina please give me another chance; I love you and I don't think I can live without you

I took another drink from the bottle and turned the music up louder.

"Oooohhhh, girl, I'll be in trouble if you left me now, 'cause I don't know where to look for love, and I don't, I don't know how!" I sang the lyrics loud, trying to hear myself over the music. I drank from the bottle again, trying to drown out my sorrows. I heard a knock on the door, but I didn't answer. The doorbell rang, followed by more knocks. Finally, I walked to the door and swung it open. I was surprised to see both my mother and my father standing there.

"Oh, Junior," my mom exclaimed as she pushed passed me. "I saw the video of Lina. Where is she?" She checked around the house, looking for Lina.

"She isn't here, Mom. She left me." My tone matched my defeated feelings.

"What the hell do you mean, she left?" She looked at me suspiciously, and I just looked away. "Adrian Nicholas Long, what did you do?" she blurted.

"Dad hired some chick to screw me, and the girl went crazy and tried to kill Lina, so she fucking left me." I said as I took another swig of the bottle. My mother glared angrily at my dad, and he looked completely confused.

"Now, Evelyn, I have no idea what is going on right now." He turned to me. "Son, what are you saying?" he asked with a puzzled look on his face. Honestly, I wanted to just slap him.

"So you're really going to sit here and act like you don't know." I said while glaring at him. He looked at me, still with lost eyes. "Hazel drugged Lina and tried to end her. You telling me you really didn't know? Get the fuck out of here, Dad!" I yelled. "All of this started when you decided I wasn't happy enough in my marriage. You hired Hazel to seduce me and take Lina's place!" My mom stared at my dad with furious eyes, and he looked away.

"That girl didn't deserve that, Adrian," she addressed her frustration toward my dad.

"I didn't know it would go that far, Eve..." My dad paused. "How was I supposed to know that she was going to go all fatal attraction on Darlina? I promise I never wanted it to go that far," he admitted and then looked at me. "I'm sorry, son. If there is anything I can do—" I cut him off.

"Dad, you have done enough. Believe me," I slurred as I finished off the bottle. "My wife has left me for another man that clearly treats her better than me." I could feel my anger build. "Are you happy now, Dad?" I asked as I pushed him.

"Son, I understand you are upset, but—" I cut him off

"Upset? You think I'm upset? I am so far past upset, Dad. I am furious." I pushed him again. "This is all your fault. You meddled instead of letting things work itself out." I pushed him again.

"Junior," my momma called out as I went to punch my dad. He blocked it and then pulled me into a hug. I tried to fight and pull my way out, but he held me tight.

"I know, son. Let it out," he comforted me as I calmed down and cried silently in his chest. My mom walked behind me and embraced me.

"We will get through this as a family," she reassured as she rubbed my back. It was at this point that I realized I was truly broken.

Hazel

I sat alone in the hospital room. I didn't have any visitors since Adrian left. That bitch Lina fucking broke my nose, and the pain was starting to kick in. I pressed the button to call the nurse. She entered the room a few minutes later with a vital machine.

"Hey, Ms. Watson." She greeted as she walked up to the bed. "So, we have to change some of your medicine," she stated as she started to take my blood pressure.

"What for?" I asked, puzzled.

"Well, your blood test came back, and congratulations, you are pregnant!" she exclaimed, and I instantly felt sick to my stomach.

"Pregnant?" I gulped, not wanting to believe the news. She nodded her head and started to hand me my medicine. I took the pills with the water she gave, and she left out of the room. "Pregnant," I said to myself, and I could feel the tears rush out of my eyes. "What the fuck—" I paused. "Wait. This might be just the thing I need to win Adrian back, and if not, this is definitely going to get me into that Long money." *I think I just hit the motherfucking jackpot. Thank you, God!*

Jaxon (Sunday Night)

I carried Lina into the crib and laid her on the couch. Walking into the kitchen, I grabbed her a cup of water so she could take her medications. Her eyes weren't as swollen anymore, and the cuts on her face were healing. I gave her the water and then walked into the bathroom and started her up a nice bath to help with her body aches. I poured some lavender bubble bath into the water and walked back out into the living room.

"You ready?" I asked as I gently lifted her off the couch. She nodded her head, and I grabbed her ponytail holder and fixed her hair into a high bun. Then I began to slowly remove her clothes, making sure not to hurt her in any way. She walked to the bathroom in just her underwear, and I followed her. She slipped off her panties, and I unsnapped her bra and helped her ease into the warm water. She moaned as she settled into the bubbles. I soaped up a washcloth and started to slowly wash her body.

This was my first time really seeing her in all her glory. She was stunning, and her skin glowed in the light. "You are so beautiful, girl," I said as I washed her back. She laid her head back, and I kissed her on the cheek. "I'm going to get the room ready for you. Call me when you are done." I got up and walked into the room. I pulled out all the candles that I had and lit them around the room. I turned the air down, so she wouldn't be cold when she walked in. I laid her out one of my T-shirts even though I didn't plan on letting her wear it.

I wanted to see all that body. I wanted to feel it next to me, so I could caress and hold on all night.

"Hud," I heard her call out, and I walked back into the bathroom with a towel. I helped her stand up and admired her dripping body. Wrapping the towel around her, I helped her out of the tub. Pulling her into an embrace, I stared deeply into her eyes, and she stared back into mine. I leaned forward and softly kissed her lips. She grabbed me by the back of my head, caressing my scalp as I slipped my tongue into her mouth. I ran my hands down her body and gripped her big, juicy booty. I could feel myself getting hard, so I pulled her closer so she could feel it too. *I have to have her.* I picked her up, and she wrapped her legs around me. I carried her into the room while our tongues rolled back and forth in each other's mouth. Laying her on the bed, I ripped open the towel and expose her beautiful body. The water glistened on her dark brown skin and I could feel myself getting more and more excited. I kissed her on her mouth again and then moved down to her neck. I kissed and sucked on both sides, making sure I left my mark.

She moaned as I trailed my tongue down to her breasts, swirling it around her right nipple as I rubbed her left one with my finger and thumb. I moved to the left breast, sucking and nibbling until she moaned in pleasure. I planted kisses down her body, pushed her legs up, and started to suck on her inner thighs. Slowly, I inched down to her beautiful succulent love box. I spread her lips and passionately kissed her insides. She moaned and grabbed my head as I sucked and licked up and down her clit.

I wanted to taste her juices. No, I needed to taste them. I slid my two fingers inside of her and slowly started to massage her G-spot. I fingered her faster, making sure I was putting more pressure on her spot each time. My lips were wrapped securely around her clit, and my tongue was darting back and forth. I was trying to give her two different orgasms at once.

"Oh my God!" she yelled as her body tensed up. Her body jerked in pleasure, and I felt her sweet nectar gush down my fingers. I pulled them out and stuck my tongue in so I could catch every drop. I stood up and pulled off my shirt. She sat up in the bed and started to undo my buckle.

She pulled down my pants, and the next thing I knew, her lips were wrapped around me. I groaned as my eyes rolled into the back of my head. Her mouth was warm and wet. I could feel my knees buckle as she slurped on my tip. I looked down, and she was rolling her head around in a circle and then bobbing up and down. *Aw shit, man.* She got this motherfucker glistening, and them damn slurping sounds are about to make me explode. Fuck it. I need her now. I pulled her up and started to kiss her in her mouth, I turned her around and pressed myself against her, I sucked on her neck and massaged her breasts.

"Jaxon, I want you to fuck me," she moaned. I bent her over the bed and slid deep inside of her, and we both let out a loud moan. *Fuck, she is wet as hell. Damn, man, I feel like I just fell into a damn water hose or something.* I pulled her up as I thrust in and out. I sucked on her neck and moaned in her ear.

"You like that?" I asked as I held her neck with one hand

and started to massage her clit with the other.

"Yes, I love it," she moaned.

"I'm about to make you cum all on this dick, girl," I teased as I began to slowly grind my hips into hers.

"No, I'm about to make you cum," she said as she turned around, pushed me on the bed, and climbed on top of me.

Lina

I slid my wet pussy on him and started to grind back and forth, making sure his dick rubbed against my G-spot. I threw my head back and started to slowly bounce up and down, making sure I took every inch. He sat up and started to kiss me. Then he grabbed my hips, helping me bounce faster. I could tell he liked to be in control, so I let him. He stood up with me on his lap, not missing a stroke as he walked over to the dresser. He sat me on top, knocking over bottles of deodorant and lotions. I arched both my legs on the dresser, rubbing my clit as he shoved himself deeper inside of me.

"Awww my God, girl, that shit is so fucking sexy." He pulled out, bent down, and stuck his tongue inside of me as I rubbed myself. I could feel his tongue slipping against my G-spot.

"Aw shit!" I yelled as I nutted all over it. He licked his lips, pulled me off the dresser, and pushed me back toward the bed.

"Get on them knees and arch that back," he said, and I did what I was told. I gasped as he pushed all of himself inside of me. "Yeah, girl, you gotta take all of this," he groaned as he smacked me on the ass. That shit turned me on, so I started to throw this ass back like it was Thursday.

"Damn, girl, that ass looking real good," he moaned as he smacked me on the butt again. Grabbing me by my hips, he started to stroke me long and hard. "I'm finna make you bust the best nut, baby," he said as he slowly started to massage my butthole with his thumb.

"Damn, that shit feels kind of good," I moaned.

"You ready, shorty?" he asked as he slowly inserted his thumb deep inside of my butt. At first, it felt weird, but I was so wet that it slipped in and out with ease. "Start rubbing that clit for me, girl," he said, and I could feel his dick pushing up against my G-spot and his thumb pushing down against it. "You like that shit, baby?" he moaned.

"Ahhhh, I love it, daddy. Please, don't fucking stop," I said as I rubbed myself.

Jaxon

Hearing her begging and calling me daddy turned me on so much that I knew I was ready to give her my all. I slammed my dick harder inside of her and pressed my thumb down into her spot. I could feel her pussy start to contract, and she let out the loudest moan of pleasure I ever heard. The shit shook me so much that I exploded deep inside of her. We both fell to the bed, panting like crazy.

"Damn, that was some good ass dick," she said as she sat up, wiping her forehead.

"I told you I was going to have you in this room begging me not to stop," I joked, and she started to laugh.

"Shut up. You know this pussy was so good you ain't want to stop."

I laughed. "Yeah, you right. Shit, I'm glad that shit is mine now," I said as I pulled her down into my arms and kissed her forehead. *She's at home now.*

Lina

I laid in the bed next to Jaxon, listening to him snore. I tossed and tuned for a few minutes before rolling over and checking the time. *Three in the morning. I wonder how Adrian is doing.* The thought ran through my mind as I remembered the pain he had in his eyes when he walked out of the hospital room. I forced Adrian out of my head when I heard Jaxon shift in the bed. I glanced over as the sheet slid of his thigh. Visions of our first time flashed through my mind and I had to catch my breath. *Damn, that sex was so fucking good. I haven't had sex like that in years,* I thought as I grabbed my phone and got out of the bed. I pulled one of Jaxon's T-shirts over my head and walked out of the room and into the kitchen. I looked around Jaxon's small apartment and instantly started to miss my nice, spacious house.

Being here made me realize that I was not just walking away from my husband; but from my house, my belongings, and just my space. *What the hell am I doing?* I could feel the tears starting up again. I know I shouldn't be this damn unhappy, because I am now out of a toxic-ass relationship, but damn, man, why am I the one going through this nonsense. I leaned on the counter, perching my arms so I could scroll through my phone. I was looking at all of the calls and messages Adrian left me.

Adrian: Lina please call me, please do not leave me, I fucking need you and I love you girl. I know I didn't treat you right, but please give me the chance to make it up to you. You are my wife; we vowed that we were in this through the good and the bad. This is just a bad patch and we can get over it, just please let me make it up to you.

That message was all it took for me to start crying uncontrollably. I threw my phone across the counter as tears rushed out of my eyes. Gripping my chest, I wailed in heartache. "Why, God!" I yelled in anger. "I was the best wife! Lord, why am I going through this shit! I did all the things I was supposed to do as a wife! How do I deserve this!" I bawled as I fell to my knees, defeated.

Jaxon

I rolled over in the bed and reached out for Lina, but she wasn't there. I fully opened my eyes, sat up, and looked around. I could hear her outside of the room, and it sounded as if she was crying. I got out of the bed, put on some underwear, and crept toward the door. I stood in the doorway, watching her scroll through her phone. *She is so fucking gorgeous. God, I just want to thank you for putting this blessing in my life. I know she is going through a storm right now, but I promise I will be her pot of gold under the rainbow.* My thoughts were interrupted by Lina throwing her phone.

"Why, God!" I could hear the anger and sadness in her voice as she pleaded to God for answers. Her pain completely filled my apartment, and my heart started to ache for her. She didn't deserve this heartache. She didn't deserve this pain. "How do I deserve this!" she cried out while falling to her knees. I could feel hot tears running down my face. I walked over to her, got down on the floor with her, and consoled her as she cried.

"You are a great wife, shorty. You just married the wrong man, and he didn't know your worth, baby girl, but I do." I rocked her as she cried in my lap. I didn't know what else to say. Really, there was nothing else left to say; the only thing left was to do. "Lina, I know it's only been a few weeks, but—"

She cut me off.

"You aren't about to propose, are you?" She sobbed as she wiped her eyes and stared directly into my face.

"No," I replied, and we stared at each other for what seemed like eternity.

"Awe, thank God," she said and started to laugh, and I laughed with her. "Boy, I was about to say." She grinned, and I wiped the rest of the tears from her face.

"OK, back to what I was saying before I was rudely interrupted," I joked as I brushed her braids out of her face. "Lina, I know it's only been a few weeks, but I can truly say that my feelings for you are real. When Jo called me and told me you were in trouble, I came running. I was ready to kill for you. Do you know why?" I asked, and she shook her head. "Because I love you. No, scratch that. I am in love with you…" I paused, waiting to hear her response, but she sat quietly.

"Hud," she finally said with a sigh, but I cut her off by putting my finger on her lips.

"Shhhh, listen, baby. I'm not saying that you should just rush and give me your heart. I'm just asking that you like me real hard." I quoted a Mario song, and she smiled, kissed me, and then climbed on top of me.

I didn't need to hear the words back, I could tell by the passion in her kiss that she felt the same way I did. She moved from my lips and started to kiss and suck on my neck. "Girl, you keep that up, and you are really gonna like me real hard," I said as my dick started to firm. She moved up to my ear and started to seductively lick my earlobe. She moaned, and that was all I needed. "You in trouble now, girl," I said as I pulled out my rock and slid it inside of her.

"Jaxon." She gasped.

"Mmmhmm, own it, baby," I said as I pulled her shirt off. "Ride this dick, girl," I moaned as she bounced up and down on my lap. I grabbed and palmed her ass cheeks as she sucked on my bottom lip.

"Oh my God," she moaned as I guided her hips back and forth. "Oh my God, Jaxon!"

"Wrap them sexy ass thighs around me and hold on to my neck." I moaned as I started to stand up, making sure our bodies never parted. I carried her over to the refrigerator and held her up against it. "Tell me you love this dick." I stroked faster as she held on to the freezer's handle, moaning. "Oh, you think I'm playing!" I yelled as I let her down, turned her around, and bent her over the counter. "Put you on the counter by the butter rolls, girl," I joked as I stroked her from the back effortlessly.

"I'm about to cum!" she yelled, and it turned me on, but I slowed down because I wanted to tease her. "Wait. Don't slow down," she pleaded as she pushed herself unto me.

"You want to cum, baby," I whispered seductively in her ear as I slowly pushed in and out of her.

"Yes!" she cried out in pleasure.

"You really want to nut, baby?" I sucked on her neck and began to slowly grind my hips into hers.

"Yes, daddy, please make me cum." She panted as I reached around her and stuck my hand in between her legs. I started to rub her clit vigorously.

"Tell me you love this dick." I started to fuck her harder and rub her clit faster. "Tell me you love this motherfucking dick, Lina!" I yelled.

"I love this motherfucking dick, Jaxon! Oh my God, I love this dick!" she yelled as her body started to shake and explode in pure ecstasy. Her warm juices gushed all down my shaft; it glistened as I slid in and out of her. She continued to shake, and her pussy continued to gush. I grabbed a hold of her breasts and pulled her closer as I let loose inside of her. I stumbled back to catch my breath, and I pulled Lina into a hug.

"I love you too, baby," I proclaimed as I kissed her on the forehead.

Four Months Later

Jaxon (12:00 a.m. Saturday)

I waited until Lina was asleep, before creeping out of the house. I had been waiting for this call for months, and I finally received it earlier tonight. I drove to the bar, parked and went inside. I ordered a drink and waited. The bar was live, the music was playing, and people were dancing and having a good time. It felt like all was right with the world.

"He will see you now," the bartender said and then started to lead me to a room in the back. I opened the door and walked in to see Jo half naked on her knees, sucking off the older gentleman that I had met here a few months ago.

"Oh, I'll come back," I said, kind of embarrassed. The older man groaned, and Jo stood up, wiping her mouth. She ran right past me without making eye contact. The gentleman stood up, fixed his pants, and walked over to the sink to wash his hands.

"Jaxon, my boy," he said as he walked over and shook my hand. "I am happy to see you. I didn't think you were going to be able to pull it off, but you did," he said as he patted me on the back.

"Now it is time for you to collect the other half of your payment." He said while grabbing his briefcase and sitting it on top of the table. I thought back to the night I met him.

"Hey, wassup?"

"Wassup, man?" I replied without making eye contact.

"It's some fine hunnies in here tonight," he stated as he turned around to face the crowd and lit a cigar that he pulled from his jacket. He was an older guy and very well dressed to be in this hole in the wall.

"Shit, the finest one just got pulled out of here," I said as I turned around and stared at the crowd myself.

"Yeah, I can tell you a lot about that one." I looked at him.

"Do tell," I said, intrigued.

"Well," he started as he blew out smoke. "She's married to my son, but I need her out of the picture," he continued, and I cut him off.

"Hey, man. I am not a killer." He laughed, but I was dead ass serious.

"I don't need you to kill her. I need you to steal her." He paused. "She is going through some things with my son, and this is the perfect chance for someone to swoop in and get her out the way so he can be more focused on what I need him to do." I looked at him.

"Is this some kind of joke?" I asked, kind of annoyed but also kind of serious.

"Far from it, and I am willing to pay you twenty-five thousand dollars now and another twenty-five thousand after she signs the divorce papers," he said as he made direct eye contact with me.

"Are you for real? But what if she doesn't leave him?" I

asked indecisively.

"Then you've made some money for your troubles of trying.
I mean, I have some other options in play already, but you can't
catch a bird with just one worm." I sat there, listening to him and
contemplating the odds. Shit seemed too damn easy but fuck it.
What did I really have to lose? I mean, shit, if I couldn't make her
fall in love with me, then I would still have this free money, and if
she does fall in love with me, then now I got the girl and the
money. What's the worst that can happen?

"Do we have a deal?" he asked with his hand out.

"Deal," I said as I placed my hand into his and shook it.

"You really did it, son," he started. "All my other players
crapped out, but you took home the prize." I looked at him.

"Who were the other players?" I asked curiously.

"One of Adrian's exes and his best friend, but they fucked
it all up," he said as he opened the briefcase. "But you did great.
You made her fall in love, she signed the papers, and I heard you
guys are expecting a baby. Shit, as the young folks say today, you
are the real MVP," he said as he turned the briefcase around,
showing me the money. "What's next? Wedding bells?" he asked,
and I picked up one of the bundles of bills.

"Yep, and a bigger place. Hell, we might even move out of
state," I said as I put the money back, closed the case, and picked it
up.

"That sounds great. Adrian is still kind of devastated by the
entire thing, but he is starting to come around, so maybe you guys

moving will be just what he needs to get back on his feet. Just remember to keep this secret in this room," he said, giving me a look,

"Believe me. I have no reason to talk about this. As far as I am concerned, you hooked me up with my soulmate," I assured.

"Well, my boy, it was a pleasure doing business with you," he said as he held out his hand.

"Same here," I said, and we shook. I turned around and left out of the backroom. The music was loud, and the atmosphere was still lit. I walked over to the bar and opened the briefcase just enough to pull out two bundles of cash. "Jo." I motioned her to come over

"Wassup, Jaxon?" she asked without making eye contact. I could tell she was ashamed.

"Hey, I am not here to judge you. You are my girl, and I just want to thank you for saving Lina's life that night." I handed her the $2,000, and she finally looked at me.

"See, I knew I always liked your ass," she said as she smiled and stuffed the money into her pants. "You might want to get out of here though," she said as she nodded toward the other end of the bar. I glanced down, and I saw Adrian sitting at the end with an empty bottle in front of him. "He's been in here every night for the past few weeks, just drinking his sorrows away," she said.

"Yeah, a few weeks ago, Lina signed the divorce because we found out she was pregnant," I said as I stood up from the bar.

"Well, congratulations on starting a new family," she said with a smile.

"Thank you. Well, let me go because I'm not with the drama." I said my goodbyes and left out of the bar. I walked to the car, put the case in the back, and closed the door.

"How's my wife?" I heard a voice slur behind me. I turned around, and Adrian was standing there with a gun pointed at me.

"Aye, man, come on. We can handle this without someone dying," I said with my hands up.

"I loved her, man, and I know I wasn't the best husband, but I didn't deserve this. You fucking stole her from me! I didn't even have a chance!" he yelled while waving the gun.

"Look, man. You and Lina wasn't meant, but this gives you the opportunity to find someone that is on the same level as you, but if you kill me, man, your entire life will be ruined," I said, trying to convince him to put the gun down. He looked at me with his finger on the trigger

"This is all your fault!" he yelled, and I closed my eyes

"Adrian!" I heard a man's voice call out as the shot rang through the air. I fell to the ground, holding my chest, but I felt no pain. My ears were ringing as I opened my eyes. I could see Adrian lying on the ground, his legs twitching on the pavement. I looked up, and his dad was standing at the door. He ran to his son.

"Adrian, son, what did you do?" He grabbed him. "Call the ambulance!" he yelled, and I pulled out my phone and called and gave them the location. I walked over to the scene, and Adrian laid there with blood spilling out of his head. I stumbled back at the sight. I got in my car and got out of there as fast as I could.

I agreed to this deal because I thought I had nothing to lose, but now an innocent life is gone, I thought I was winning $50,000 for free, but now I know everything comes with a price, and the price I have to live with is guilt, and I just pray to God it doesn't eat me alive. I pulled up to the house. I couldn't get the sound of Adrian's leg scraping across the ground out of my head. I walked into the house and hid the briefcase with the other money. I got undressed in the living room and quietly stepped into the bedroom. Lina laid sleeping in the bed. She was already beautiful, but the pregnancy glow made her gorgeous. I got in the bed and cuddled up next to her.

For her sake, I have to bottle in these emotions and be all I can be for her and this baby. I moved closer and rubbed her stomach. Adrian shooting himself is not my fault; the only fault I have is loving a woman that needed to be loved, and I will continue to love her to infinity and beyond. I closed my eyes. *Tomorrow begins a new day.*

Next Book To Read:
Jaded

(use to be titled "Nice for What 2)

Made in the USA
Monee, IL
10 June 2022